Adven
Sa

Secret

Adventures
on the
Santa Lucia
Secret Persuader

Pamela Oldfield

An Armada Original

Secret Persuader was first published in Armada in 1989

Armada is an imprint of the Children's Division,
part of the Collins Publishing Group,
8 Grafton Street, London W1X 3LA

Printed and bound in Great Britain by
William Collins Sons & Co. Ltd, Glasgow

One

Ann stood at the rail with Jay beside her and together they watched the quayside slide away from the ship. Ann was nearly fourteen with straight brown hair, cut very short, grey eyes and a resourceful expression. Her brother, Jason, took after his father with short-sighted brown eyes and dark curly hair. He was nearly nine. Actually, of course, it was the ship that was moving as the luxury cruise ship *Santa Lucia*, left Southampton for her transatlantic crossing. In five days time they would dock in New York Harbour and the holiday would be over. Ann sighed as she watched a seagull alight on the green water far below them. If only their mother could have been with them it would have been perfect but that could not be. Their parents were divorced and Ann and Jay shared their time between their English mother and their American father.

"This your first time on the *Santa Lucia*?"

She glanced sideways to see a tall boy of about her own age grinning in a friendly way. He was casually dressed in jeans and a grey sweat shirt and his freckled face was topped by a mass of tousled fair hair. He spoke with a distinctive American drawl and Ann guessed that he was from one of the southern states of America.

"No," she answered, returning his smile. "We often do it. My father won't let us fly because his brother died in a plane crash. He lives in New York and my mother lives in Hastings."

Jay joined in the conversation. "We go backwards and forwards," he said. "Like yo-yos. D'you know where Hastings is?"

"No, but I guess it's in England."

"It's in Kent," Jay told him, "on the south coast. We spend all of August with our mother. It's great."

The boy nodded. "Well, this is my first trip," he told them. "We flew over in Concorde. Now we're going home. My name's Luke – Luke Carter."

"I'm Ann and he's Jay," said Ann. "Our father is Art Burnside."

Luke's eyes widened. "The cookery guy?"

"Yes. He's in Morocco right now but he'll be back in New York by the time we get there."

Jay piped up. "So he says. Last time he was late getting back and Ann did the cooking. Ugh!" He held his stomach and groaned horribly.

"Charming!" exclaimed Ann, with mock indignation. "You can cook your own food next time."

"I will," said Jay loftily.

No one could call Jay shy. He had an outgoing

personality, with plenty of self-confidence and he found life a great adventure.

On shore the band was playing a selection of sea shanties as the tugs eased the huge liner away from the dockside. Next to Luke a plump elderly woman clutched at her hat with a hand that glittered with diamond rings.

Suddenly she turned to Luke. "I do so hope we have a smooth crossing. I'm such a poor sailor. Have you heard the weather forecast, by any chance?"

Luke shook his head but Ann said. "Today and tonight will be fine but tomorrow's not so good. But don't worry too much. She's such a big ship she can ride most seas."

"And she's got sterilizers," said Jay. "The steward told me."

"He means stabilizers," Ann told her. "To stop her from rolling."

"I hope you're right. I do hate to be seasick," she said. "All that wonderful food and you can't manage a mouthful."

Her pink dress matched her shoes and her straw hat was a mass of feathers. All her clothes were obviously very expensive and Ann felt that all she needed to complete the picture was a small dog tucked under her arm.

"My late husband used to tease me about my appetite but I always told him – Food is one of life's little luxuries. With some people it's fast cars or horses. With me it's food. I just love to eat. I appreciate good cooking the way some people enjoy good paintings."

Jay was giving her a long stare but suddenly he decided he had heard enough from this weird lady.

"I'm going down to the games room," he told Ann. "See you later, alligator."

As they watched him go Ann grinned. "That games room!" she said. "He *lives* there. Dad says there ought to be a government warning on the door – Non-stop video is bad for your health!"

The plump woman in pink nodded vaguely then wandered away, still clutching her hat, and Ann smiled.

"Poor thing," she said. "I hope she doesn't get seasick. I was trying to reassure her but actually it can be very rough if the wind gets up. If the dining room stewards take the flowers off the tables, watch out!"

Luke frowned. "I don't get that. What do flowers have to do with anything?"

"Well, the flowers are in tall silver vases and they can easily topple over, so when the stewards know that bad weather is on the way they remove them. If they remove the water jugs as well . . ." She laughed expressively.

"Time to batten down the hatches," he said. "I get it." They both laughed.

"Are you travelling alone?" Ann asked.

"No, I'm with my stepfather," Luke explained. "We just 'did' Europe in six weeks. Ma thought I needed a bit of culture. London, Rome, Vesuvius, Pompeii, Athens, Paris, the Eiffel Tower— "

"All in six weeks!" gasped Ann. "You must be shattered."

"I am," he confessed, "but not Sven. That's my stepfather. He's Danish. He took it all in his stride. He's amazing."

He explained that his real father had died and his mother had then married a much older man. Sven Hannsen was nearly seventy but had surprising energy.

"Where is he now?"

Luke grinned. "Right now I guess he's in the gym and then he'll take a sauna. First thing in the morning he'll be jogging round the deck. I like him a lot. He's never been married before and he doesn't really know what to do with a family. He's very fond of us, but he just carries on as though he's still a bachelor."

At that moment the ship's orchestra began to play as the liner pulled further away from the docks. A group of people next to Ann were hurling streamers into the water and everywhere cameras flashed and video cameras whirred.

"Well," said Ann, straightening up from the ship's rail. "I suppose I'll have to unpack, but it's so boring.

9

Still the sooner it's over the better. We might bump into each other later on – at dinner maybe. Where do you eat? We're travelling transatlantic class so we're in the *Santa Lucia* restaurant."

"We're in the Lucia Grill Room," he said.

"Oh! You really *are* rich!" she teased. "What does Sven do for a living?"

"Was in oil," grinned Luke. "Need I say more?"

"Not a word!" said Ann and as they went their separate ways, she made up her mind to meet him again sometime.

The F deck cabin she shared with Jay was small but comfortably furnished with two beds separated by a dressing table. The green carpet matched the bed covers and there was a stool and an easy chair. There was also a roomy wardrobe and a full length mirror. A small door in one corner of the room led into the bathroom. It was an inside cabin so there was no porthole.

To Ann the cabin was like a second home and she quickly unpacked her clothes and then turned her attention to a number of leaflets which lay on the dressing table. There was a "Welcome aboard" message from the captain and a list of entertainments planned for the rest of the day. Ann read them quickly and then threw herself cheerfully onto the bed. Five whole days, she thought, to get to know Luke. It would be fun to have a companion of her own age. She went to the wardrobe and chose jazzy,

10

calf-length trousers and a baggy shocking pink tee shirt. One way or another she was looking forward to the trip. It was always great fun.

That evening, Ann and Jay went into dinner and found themselves as usual at a table for six.

The restaurant was a vast, airy room full of circular tables. At intervals there were service stations of stainless steel to which the food was delivered from the galley before it was served to the diners.

To their delight their table stewards were Tony and Simon, whom they had met on the voyage over.

"You two here again?" Tony asked with a smile as he handed them their menus. He was tall and slim with grey eyes.

"We could ask the same about you," said Jay cheekily.

Ann groaned. "Who is this awful brat?" she asked. "He's nothing to do with me."

The steward laughed. "I'm here because I'm the best," he told Jay. "It's as simple as that."

"And they can't let me go," said Simon as he offered them a basket of bread rolls, "because I'm too good looking." He was shorter than his colleague with wavy brown hair, a small moustache and a cheerful face.

"And modest with it!" said Ann. "What sort of crossing are we going to have? Any idea?"

11

"Ah!" Tony rolled his eyes dramatically. "My lips are sealed," he said.

Jay gave a screech of exaggerated horror. "I know what *that* means," he said. "It means you know it's going to be awful but you aren't telling."

Tony shrugged. "Mustn't spread gloom and despondency," he said. "Now are you ready to give your orders, sir and madame?" They were not in the least ready so the stewards moved on to another table while Ann and Jay studied the menu with great concentration. There was a bewildering choice of delicious food, with special selections for children and people who were slimming. Jay, Ann knew, would choose sausage, baked beans and chips, which was his stock favourite.

"I think I'll have almond soup," she said, "and the Chicken Kiev."

"Oh no!" cried Jay, crinkling his nose. "That means you'll stink of garlic."

"Hard cheese!" said Ann. "You'll stink of sausage, baked beans and chips!"

At that moment a tall thin man came up to their table and sat down opposite them. He gave Ann's pink tee shirt a disapproving look but made no effort to introduce himself. He busied himself with his table napkin and poured himself a glass of water. Ann watched him out of the corner of her eye and decided that she did not like him.

"He looks kind of creepy," she thought but then

12

told herself not to be silly. But his manner was pre-occupied and there was an expression in his eyes that made her feel vaguely uneasy. She was relieved when the last three people joined the table – a mother and father with their talkative middle-aged daughter who told them they were on their way to visit cousins in Milwaukee. They introduced themselves as John and Mabel Hubbard and the daughter as Alice Paine.

They all did their best to include the tall man in the conversation but after reluctantly disclosing his name, which was Adam May, he relapsed once more into a stony silence. He chose salad and smoked salmon, pushed it around his plate without eating very much of it and then made an abrupt excuse and left the table.

"Good riddance to bad rubbish," muttered Jay and Ann kicked him under the table. But no one was sorry to see him go and the meal proceeded much more happily without him. When they had finished their coffee, Ann and Jay left the restaurant and Jay departed once more for the games room. Ann paused in the lounge. Later there would be dancing, a singer and a comedian but she had decided instead to call in at the ship's library and look for a book to take back to her cabin. To her delight she found Luke there accompanied by an elderly blond man whose face lit up as she greeted Luke.

"Ah! You must be Anna," he said. "My favourite name." He seized her hand in a grip of iron and began to pump it up and down with great enthusiasm. He looked no more than fifty-five, Ann thought, astonished.

"It's not Anna, it's *Ann*," Luke told him.

"My stepson is telling me all about you," said Sven, finally releasing her hand. He spoke English with a Scandinavian accent. "You like to walk with me?" he asked her. "I am promising myself five more miles to – how you say? – 'walk off' my too big dinner. Luke here, he will not come. He is what his mother calls a 'book worm'. No?"

"Yes," said Luke. "At least, I prefer reading to hiking!"

"And you, Anna?" asked Sven.

Luke shrugged good-naturedly, giving up the struggle with Ann's name.

"I think I'm too lazy," she confessed with a smile, "although I might go for a swim tomorrow."

"Do you play the deck quoits?" he persisted. Ann shook her head.

"I could teach you. We could go now to the deck."

"That's very kind but – " She looked appealingly at Luke who promptly came to her rescue.

"Ann's tired," he suggested. "Maybe tomorrow we'll both join you in the pool."

Sven's face broke into a smile. "That would be very good," he said. "Tomorrow we shall see. Now, I must walk. The coffee gateau was a mistake and always we must pay for our mistakes. Is it not so?"

14

Ann agreed and watched as Sven made his way out of the library with a cheerful word for everyone he passed. When he had gone Ann and Luke turned to the well-stocked shelves. They were still poring over the rows of books when the plump lady they had met earlier came into the library. She was now dressed in pale blue and she passed Ann and Luke without recognizing them. Ann caught sight of a small round patch of sticking plaster just behind her right ear and for some reason which she could not explain, the sight of it sent a shudder down her spine.

Two

Next morning at breakfast the vase of flowers was missing from the table and Ann caught Simon's eye.

"Don't tell me," she said. "I don't want to know!"

He shrugged. "The wind's getting up so my advice is eat a good breakfast. You know what I told you last time."

She nodded. "Line your stomach," she said. "Well, in that case I'll have egg and bacon please, followed by toast and marmalade."

"Where's that terrible brother of yours? Isn't he coming in to breakfast."

"I haven't a clue," said Ann. "He rushed off for a quick game of Space Invaders before I was properly awake but – Ah!" She broke off. "Here he comes now."

Jay darted eagerly around the more sedate passengers who were also arriving for breakfast. His dark hair was dishevelled and his tee shirt was on back to front.

"Jay!" she groaned. "You look like a proper scrumbag!"

It was strange, she reflected, how different they were. He was very bright and bubbling over with confidence while she was much quieter. She had been an only child for five years and when promised a playmate, had somehow expected a sister. Her disappointment had been terrible. She had refused even to look at him for the first few weeks of his life! Now she could not imagine life without him.

While Jay was ordering his breakfast, the Hubbards arrived with their daughter. Mabel looked rather pale.

"Is it my imagination," she said, "or is the sea getting rougher? I must admit I feel rather queasy this morning."

Ann repeated the steward's advice about lining the stomach but Mabel looked doubtful. She managed a few mouthfuls of toast and a cup of tea but then gave up.

Adam May did not appear at all but no one minded since he had not proved a very cheerful companion.

After breakfast Ann and Jay had met up with Sven and Luke and together the four of them browsed in the shopping arcade that ran around the gallery above the main lounge. Jay bought a small paperweight as a present for his father and Luke chose a headscarf for his mother. Ann was looking through the postcards when she noticed Adam May, deep in conversation with the plump, elderly woman who

17

loved eating. Ann watched them curiously because they seemed such an ill-assorted pair, one large and talkative, the other slim and withdrawn. Several times the woman put a hand to the right side of her neck and Ann wondered if she was explaining the reason for the small circular patch. Deliberately Ann drifted a little nearer to overhear their conversation.

"I do hope you're right," the woman was saying, "because the room steward tells me the weather is definitely deteriorating. At the moment I feel just rather woozy, as though I'm only half awake."

"That will wear off," he said. "Try to relax. Forget all about it. Don't talk about it to anyone."

"You're not wearing one yourself, I notice," she said. "Why's that? Surely you should – "

But he had caught sight of Ann and he now put a finger to his lips to silence the old woman and answered her in lowered tones.

"'Morning Mr May," said Ann brightly. "And Mrs – " she smiled at the woman. "I don't know your name. I'm Ann. Ann Burnside."

The woman said, "I'm Hettie Bell. That's my late husband's name. Poor Edgar, he so wanted a trip on the *Santa Lucia* but business is business and he always had to fly to and fro. So much quicker, of course, but not half so much fun." Her plump fingers strayed once more to the neat circle on her neck. "I was just saying to Mr May – " she began, but with

18

a warning look and a muttered excuse, Adam May abruptly left them.

"Well, that beats everything," said Mrs Bell, staring after him. "He is just the strangest man. So considerate in some respects but entirely lacking in social graces." She lowered her voice and touched the patch on her neck. "Has he told you, honey, about these?"

"No, he hasn't," said Ann. "What are they?"

"They are the very latest anti-seasickness drug," Mrs Bell explained. "And rather exclusive, if you take my meaning."

"I don't think I do."

Mrs Bell leaned towards her confidentially. "Well, honey, they're so new they're not generally available to the public. The point is, that they're a hundred per cent effective but very expensive. I mean, *real* expensive. The average person could never afford them so they are only being offered to a select few. Mr May mentioned them to me yesterday evening and of course I went straight to the ship's doctor and asked for one. But we're not supposed to talk about it."

Ann frowned. "I don't get it," she said. "How does it work exactly?"

Mrs Bell raised plump shoulders in a shrug. "Well, it's like this. The patch is impregnated with the drug and the drug is slowly absorbed into the blood stream through the skin. You couldn't take it all in one dose

19

because it's so powerful. Something of that kind. The doctor was such a lamb, he explained it in words of one syllable but I do forget these things. Brain like a sieve, Edgar used to say, but then he liked dumb blondes. 'Never marry a woman who's brighter than you are,' he used to say. Can you imagine that?"

"What's it called, this drug?" Ann asked. "Can you remember?"

Mrs Bell looked embarrassed. "Oh look honey, I doubt if you could afford it."

"Oh, don't worry, I never get seasick," Ann told her. "I'm just interested, that's all."

The old lady frowned. "It was a long name. Something like alphamenobenzine – no, that's not quite it. Alphabymenzodrine? No. It was alpha something – I'm sure of that, but the rest escapes me, I'm afraid."

"And how d'you feel? Is it working?"

"I feel rather light-headed, to tell you the truth. I was just telling Mr May. I'm going to find a deck lounger and relax in the lido. The breeze makes it rather chilly on deck."

When Mrs Bell had gone, Luke came up to Ann and she told him briefly what she had learned.

"Perhaps I should tell Sven about the drug," he said. "He's not a very good sailor. I tease him about it because he's Danish. All those Viking ancestors, I tell him, and you don't even have sea legs!"

Jay had disappeared to the games room by this time and Sven had gone up on deck to walk off his breakfast. Ann and Luke went to look at the list of events which was posted on the wall near the library. "There's a lecture on photography at 10.30 in the theatre," said Luke. "Fancy that?"

"No," said Ann, "but there's a quiz in the Queen's Room at the same time. I rather like quizzes although I never know any of the answers. We could go separately and meet up later." She made the suggestion but really she was hoping they would stay together.

"Let's try the quiz," grinned Luke. "I'm feeling rather knowledgeable this morning."

Promptly at half past ten one of the ship's entertainment officers appeared to organize the event and everyone who wanted to take part was given a sheet of paper on which to write down the answer to the questions. On the other side of the room Ann spotted Mabel and John Hubbard, but their daughter was no longer with them.

The questions were varied. "What is the capital of Australia?" "Who wrote *Gone with the Wind*?" "What is a fingerling?"

"I hardly know any of the answers," Ann whispered. "I knew I wouldn't."

"I don't know many either," Luke confessed, but somehow it did not seem to matter.

When the questions had all been read out the participants changed papers with someone nearby and the marking began. To Ann's surprise, Mabel was declared the winner and was awarded a medallion to mark her success.

Ann and Luke then decided to go for a swim before lunch and, as they expected, they found Sven already in the pool. He waved to them cheerfully before plunging once more into the water.

"He's fantastic!" said Ann. "I hope I'm as fit as he is when I'm seventy."

"You think you're going to last that long?" asked Luke.

"I'm going to try," she told him and gave him a push that sent him backwards into the pool.

The water was comfortably warm and for the best part of an hour they swam and splashed about. There were never more than a dozen people swimming at one time and Ann was able to practise a racing plunge under Sven's capable tuition. Because they were in the water, they did not notice the movement of the ship but as soon as they climbed out they realized that the weather had worsened.

"I hope I'm not going to be seasick," said Luke as they made their way somewhat erratically back to their respective cabins.

That afternoon the wind increased, the ship began to roll more noticeably and people began to look anxiously out of the windows at the dark clouds which now raced ominously across the sky. The captain's champagne reception was to be held in the evening and most of the passengers were looking forward to changing from their casual clothes into something more formal. Luke informed Ann that he would be totally unrecognizable in a dark jacket and bow tie while Sven would be in full evening dress.

"Thanks for the warning," Ann laughed. "I may condescend to get out of my shorts and tee shirt for a few hours but I'll have a job to get Jay into anything reasonable."

She was absolutely right. Not only did Jay decline to wear anything smart but he refused point blank to attend the reception at all.

"They won't give us any champagne and orange juice is dead boring!" he argued.

Ann was delighted. It would be much more fun, she thought, if she went to the reception on her own, so she willingly left Jay to his own devices. She wore a blue and white calf-length skirt and new blue sweater and made her way up in the lift to the reception. The captain was waiting to shake hands with her as another officer asked her name and boomed it out for everyone to hear.

"Miss Ann Burnside!"

As she shook hands the captain smiled and joked. "You are becoming one of our regulars, Miss Burnside."

The photographer leaned forward and recorded the handshake on film but he, too, recognized her and knew that she no longer bought the photographs of herself shaking hands with the captain. As soon as she was past the photographer a steward appeared at her elbow with a tray of glasses and she was soon seated beside one of the coffee tables sipping a glass of Perrier water and trying to pretend it was champagne. She was looking round hopefully for Luke and Sven when Mrs Bell appeared. She was staggering slightly as she walked towards Ann but only with the motion of the ship.

"Isn't this embarrassing!" she cried as she flopped down on to the seat beside Ann. "I feel quite drunk, tottering about like this, and yet I haven't had a single drink. I don't seem to enjoy my food so much since this – " She tapped the patch. "And I'm not at all sure that it's working properly. I think I do feel rather sick and I've the strangest sensation in my head."

"Like what?" Ann asked her.

"Well, I know this will sound absurd but I feel as though someone is trying to tell me something but I can't quite grasp it. Like a faint voice on the telephone when the line's bad. You know what I mean? Does that sound too ridiculous?"

"It sounds weird," Ann agreed.

Mrs Bell sipped her champagne and wrinkled her nose. "I can't seem to taste things properly or hear things properly – I suppose it's what they call a side effect. I wonder if any of the others are experiencing the same problems."

24

"How many other people have this alpha thing?"

Mrs Bell shrugged. "Maybe half a dozen," she said. "I noticed Horace Keston, the wealthy industrialist – he's wearing one – and Lady Rothford, widow of Lord James Rothford who owns a chain of cinemas and – " She broke off suddenly and her eyes narrowed anxiously. "It's happening again," she whispered. "Oh, what *is* he saying? I feel it's important that I should know."

"Know what?" asked Ann and she was touched by the cold finger of fear she had felt earlier.

"Hush!"

Ann saw panic in Mrs Bell's blue eyes as she tried desperately to decipher her "message".

"No," she sighed at last with a shake of her head. "I nearly had it then but now it's gone. I feel sure I have to do something, but what?"

Ann looked at her with growing concern. Was the old lady delirious, perhaps? Had the new drug made her ill?

"Mrs Bell, are you O.K.?" she asked.

To her surprise, Mrs Bell looked at her blankly. "Well, of course I'm all right. Why do you ask?"

"But that voice you hear inside your head – the one telling you to do something. Shouldn't you see the doctor?"

Suddenly Mrs Bell put a hand to her forehead and winced.

"It hurts," she groaned and clasped her head with both hands. "Oh, it hurts!"

A voice made them both jump.

"Go to your cabin, Mrs Bell, and lie down."

As Ann turned to see Adam May behind them, Mrs Bell rose obediently to her feet.

"What's the matter with her?" said Ann.

He ignored her. "It's best for you to rest," he told the old lady. "I will help you to your cabin."

"Oh, but I don't want to trouble you – " Mrs Bell began.

"It's no trouble," he said firmly. "Take my arm."

"My head hurts!" she groaned. "Yes, I think I should like to lie down. But – " She looked at Adam May, dismayed. "The number of my cabin! I've completely forgotten it. And it was such an easy number to remember. Oh dear! I'm being such a nuisance but my head feels so strange."

"Don't worry," he told her. "I know your cabin number. Take my arm, Mrs Bell."

Mrs Bell nodded without further protest and with a sinking heart Ann watched them walk away together, stumbling a little with the roll of the ship.

"How on earth did he know her cabin number?" Ann asked herself.

The more she thought about it, the more certain she became that something very odd was happening to Mrs Bell.

"Very odd and very unpleasant," she muttered.

26

"And I'd like to know what it is! I shall keep a sharp eye on you, Mr May. You're up to something and I'm going to find out what it is."

Three

Adam May did not appear at dinner, and neither did Mabel Hubbard.

"Feeling a bit under the weather," John confided. "She couldn't face the full meal but the steward brought her some chicken sandwiches. I hope she'll be able to keep them down."

Ann was glad that Adam May was not dining with them. Her earlier impression of him had changed from dislike into mistrust and she did not at all relish his company. Yet nor could she enjoy his absence because she had the uneasy feeling that wherever he was he was up to no good.

After dinner she found Luke and she persuaded him to go up on deck where they would not be overheard and while they walked she shared her suspicions with him. She told him of her recent encounter with Mrs Bell and went on.

"I know it sounds crazy but I've got a very bad feeling about him. Bad vibrations, as they say. I don't think he's just antisocial at mealtimes. I think he's got something on his mind and he's so wrapped up in whatever it is, he hardly knows we exist."

To her relief, he did not laugh as she had feared he would but listened very carefully until she had finished and then nodded.

"You may be right," he said. "Sven thinks he recognizes him. We've passed him several times and every time Sven says 'I know this face. Where have I seen this face before?' It really seems to bother him because he can't remember."

"And he has no idea at all?"

"No – except that Sven thinks his name begins with a 'B'."

"But his name's Adam May."

"So he tells us."

Ann stared at him. "You mean he's changed his name?"

"Could be. If, as you think, he's up to something crooked he'd hardly be using his real name. At least, not if he had any sense."

"And not if it was a name people might remember for some reason!"

They stopped walking and stared at one another. An elderly man approached on the arm of a younger man and Ann and Luke moved aside to let them pass then leaned together on the ship's rail.

"Suppose," said Ann slowly, "that he once did something criminal and had his photograph in the paper— "

"Or was on T.V!"

"Then *we* would remember him," said Ann. "Unless— "

"Unless it was years ago when we wouldn't have seen it but Sven would!" said Luke. "I think that's it. If only Sven could remember a bit more about him."

For a while they were busy with their own thoughts then Ann said. "It was so frightening the way Mrs Bell *listened* for that voice in her head."

"Maybe it was her conscience," grinned Luke, then seeing Ann's expression he said. "Sorry, just fooling."

But Ann was deep in thought again. "Another thing," she said. "I noticed today how many people are wearing those same patches."

A gleam came into her eyes and she turned excitedly to Luke.

"Look, we think the drug in the patch is affecting Mrs Bell's mind. We also think that whatever cures the seasickness has a bad side effect. If we want to know a bit more about those patches why don't I go to the ship's doctor and ask for one? We know he'll say 'No' because they're so expensive but it would be interesting to see what he says about them."

Luke looked at her doubtfully. "It's a bit risky," he said. "If one of us has to go it should be me."

Ann tossed her head indignantly. "I don't see why," she said. "It was my idea. Anyway you *are* rich so if you ask for a patch he just might give you one. Then *you* might hear voices."

He frowned. "I don't think he'd give me one," he said slowly. "Most of the people who wear them are elderly – but that might be because people get richer as they get older."

"Or they're more easily coaxed out of their money," Ann suggested. "More willing to part with their money for something that doesn't even work very well."

"Who says it doesn't?"

"Mrs Bell. She said at the reception that she was feeling a bit sick yet she was one of the first to wear a patch." Ann straightened up. "It was my idea so I shall go," she said firmly.

Luke did not look too happy. "Go on then," he said, "but I'm coming with you. I'll hang around just out of sight."

The decision made, they set off for the doctor's surgery. As Ann knocked at the half open door her heart was beating a little faster than usual. A middle-aged nurse looked up from her desk and smiled cheerfully.

"It's Miss Burnside, isn't it?" she said. "The young lady who tried to drown herself in the swimming pool."

Ann laughed. "That was years ago!" she protested. "And I *didn't* try to drown myself. I banged heads with someone under water and knocked myself out! No one will let me forget it."

"It gave us quite a fright, though," said the nurse.

"But now, what can we do for you? Surely after all the crossings you've made you're not feeling queasy."

Ann wished she had had the sense to think up a convincing lie.

"I just want to see the doctor," she said. "It's well – I can't explain it. It's rather personal."

"Oh, I see," said the nurse, making it quite clear by her tone of voice that she did not see. "Well, go straight in."

Ann pushed open the door. The doctor was relocking a small wall cabinet but he turned and smiled at her. He was small, plump and balding with rosy cheeks and a good-humoured face.

"Miss Burnside!" he said. "The *Santa Lucia* must feel like your second home."

"It does," said Ann.

"How many crossings have you made now?"

"Eighteen – maybe nineteen. I forget exactly."

"And how can I help you?"

Ann took a deep breath. "I've been talking to people about those seasickness patches," she said. "I'd really like to try it, if they're not too expensive."

"You!" he exclaimed. "Seasick? I don't believe it!"

"I know," Ann stammered. "It's really stupid after all these years but – " She shrugged, leaving the sentence unfinished. "I know they're called alpha–something – and they're terribly powerful. I've never heard of them before. Just a small round patch.

32

It's marvellous. So simple."

"Anaphetabenzilene, to be correct," he said. "And yes, it's very new. It's only just come off the research list and Mr May assures us it will prove quite revolutionary."

"Mr May?" echoed Ann, surprised. "Adam May, do you mean?"

"Yes. Adam May. He's one of the firm's top agents. They are just beginning to put it on the market and we on the *Santa Lucia* are privileged to be among the first to try it out. But it *is* expensive because some of the ingredients are quite rare." He smiled. "I think it's probably beyond your pocket, Miss Burnside."

She tried to look disappointed. "Oh? How much is it exactly?" she asked.

He smiled. "Does five hundred dollars sound a lot of money to you?"

"Five hundred dollars! Holy Moses!"

"You see why we aren't advertising it widely. It would upset the passengers to know that there's a brilliant new cure available which they can't afford. Hopefully, in time, the drug house will find a way of bringing down the cost but that's not likely just yet."

Ann nodded, thinking frantically. There would be no other chance to talk to the doctor and she wondered what else she should ask.

"Who makes it?" she asked. "Would I know them?"

33

"Hemmel and Wizeman, but I don't suppose that means much to you."

She was forced to admit that it meant nothing at all.

"So how does anyone on the *Santa Lucia* know it's available?" she persisted.

Suddenly he looked rather sheepish. "Ah, that was Mr May's idea," he told her. "He studied the passenger list and only approaches people who can obviously afford it." He drew his brows together, obviously becoming puzzled by her continued interest. "The man you should really be talking to is Mr May," he told her. "He knows all the answers whereas I only know what he has told me. I just dispense them. I'm not an expert."

Ann pricked up her ears. "Hasn't this firm told you anything, then? This Hemmel and Wizeman?"

"They didn't need to," he said defensively. "They were sending their top agent to work with me. Anyway, I really don't see – "

Too late, Ann realized that she had asked one too many questions.

"I'm sorry, doctor," she said quickly. "But please could you write down that name for me. Jay, my little brother, loves long words." She managed a light laugh. "He'll put it in his collection."

Hardly bothering to hide his irritation, the doctor wrote the name on the top sheet of a handy prescription pad and handed it to her.

"Thank you," she said, folding it quickly and pushing it into her pocket. "I'll leave you in peace now."

"But I thought you felt seasick," he protested. "Don't you want to try something else? I can give you an injection. That's only eight dollars and they're reasonably effective."

Ann hastily declined the offer, saying she hoped she would get over it.

"Come back if you change your mind," he said and a moment later she was back in the corridor with Luke.

Together they made their way back to the boat deck and there they discussed all the new information she had gleaned from the doctor. They were forced to admit that it certainly sounded a very plausible story. Why, then, did they still feel so uneasy?

Ann shrugged her shoulders. "Maybe I've been making a mountain out of a molehill," she said. "When I think about it logically it all makes sense so there *can't* be anything sinister going on. I mean, the doctor wouldn't be in on any kind of plot, I'm sure of that. He's been with this ship for years. Everyone likes him."

Luke nodded. "And I guess Adam May has to be genuine if Hemmel and Wizeman sent him to the *Santa Lucia*. I guess it makes sense. We'll have to let it go."

"I suppose so," Ann agreed reluctantly. "If only

it wasn't for Mrs Bell and that voice of hers, telling her to *do* something. That's what's so creepy – and nothing the doctor said explains that."

"Hold it a minute!" cried Luke with a snap of his fingers. "Who says the voice has to be connected with the patch? Say she was like that *before* she came on the ship. Maybe she's a little wacky and hears voices all the time!"

Ann considered the possibility for a few moments. "If so," she said slowly, "then there's nothing wrong at all."

"All a figment of your imagination!" he grinned.

For another full minute Ann hesitated, checking and rechecking all that she had learned against her earlier suspicions. Finally she was forced to laugh at herself.

"O.K. I'm an idiot!" she said. "I made two and two make five!"

"Don't be too hard on yourself," said Luke. "It did look kind of fishy."

Ann drew a deep breath. "Then we can forget all about it," she said. "Poor Mr May. There's me casting him as the villain when all the time he's perfectly innocent." She put two fingers to the side of her forehead and said "Bang!"

Luke glanced at his watch. "I vote we go to the movie. It starts in exactly seven minutes and goes on until past eleven, but who cares."

"I don't," said Ann.

"What about Jay?"

"What about him. He'll be O.K. He'll go back to the cabin soon after nine. I'll slip out of the film later and check that he's there."

"What are we waiting for then? Let's get down to the theatre."

Four

Later that night the weather grew worse and the sea became very rough indeed. Ann woke to find Jay sitting up in his bunk wide-eyed and excited.

"Wake up!" he told her. "The ship's bucking about like a crazy horse. I thought I was going to fall out of bed!" Even as he spoke the ship rolled to starboard and all the objects on the dressing table slid down to one end and fell off onto Jay's bed.

"Must be a storm?" Ann suggested.

"I think it's a typhoon – or a hurricane. Maybe the ship will get sucked up into the air in a giant waterspout!"

He began to return all the objects to the dressing table – Ann's watch, the paperweight, the room key and a few coins.

"It's just a storm," Ann told him. "A double jumbo storm."

"When is a storm not a storm," he asked. "When it's a hurricane."

Just then the ship ploughed headlong into a particularly ferocious wave and the cabin did indeed seem to be lifted as though by giant hands and dropped just as suddenly. Jay made the most of it, hurling himself out of bed and onto the floor.

"Wow!" cried Jay. "This is smashing! This is the best trip ever!"

The ship settled for less than a minute before rolling again, this time to port and Jay laughed as the contents of the dressing table slid onto Ann's bed. Ann collected them up. "That's enough of that," she said. "I'll put them in a carrier bag until the storm is over. Otherwise they'll fall on us every time the ship rolls."

There was a crash from the bathroom. "Oh, what was that?"

"The toothbrush mugs fell into the basin," said Jay. They went to investigate and, as Jay had predicted, the toothmugs were indeed in the basin. Fortunately, they were made of plastic or they would have smashed. The toothpaste and the brushes were on the floor.

Eventually, they had all the movable objects around the cabin stowed safely away and they settled down in their beds once more.

Ann knew from past experience that during bad weather an inside cabin on deck five was the best place to be because the centre of the ship had a shorter distance to roll. She wondered what it must be like for Sven and Luke? They had a first class stateroom near the bow of the ship

– ideal in fine weather but very vulnerable in a storm.

"Rather them than me," she thought drowsily. But the storm had not reached its peak and they slept only fitfully for the rest of the night and were glad when scurrying feet in the corridor outside told them that it was morning.

When they went in to breakfast they found that they were the only people at the table.

"Trust you two to make it!" Simon joked as he took their orders. "How did you sleep?"

"With difficulty!" Ann grinned.

Jay's eyes gleamed. "I was thrown out of bed!" he cried. "Crash! Onto the floor. I nearly broke my leg!"

Simon assumed an expression of great concern. "Nearly broke your leg? How terrible."

"It was pretty awful," said Ann, "and it's not much better now. What on earth is happening?"

"We've had problems," Simon told them. "The captain was trying to avoid a hurricane so he changed course and we sailed due south. Unfortunately, we just caught the tail end of it. Now we have to change course again to make our way back to New York."

"That was the *tail end* of a hurricane!" said Ann. "I'm glad we didn't catch all of it."

"I told you!" Jay gloated. "I said it was a hurricane."

40

Ann looked round at the rest of the dining room and saw that it was only half full.

"So, is the worst over?" she asked.

"My lips are sealed," Simon told her.

Jay's eyes widened. "That means it's not!" he gasped. "That means it's going to get worse. We'll capsize. I bet we will. We'll have to be rescued. Women and children first . . ."

He broke off as the ship tilted alarmingly. Simon managed to steady himself but another steward who was passing lost his balance and fell, taking a tray of clean plates with him. There was a tremendous crash.

Simon smiled. "He's new," he said as the young man scrambled to his feet red-faced but unhurt and began to gather up the broken crockery. "This is his first crossing."

"Poor man," said Ann. "He's probably wishing he'd decided to be a brain surgeon instead."

"I'll be a ship's steward when I grow up," said Jay. "It looks like fun." He applied himself to the menu once more. "Please can I have banana on my cornflakes?"

"Certainly, sir," said Simon. "Ah, here comes Tony. I thought perhaps we'd lost him overboard!"

Tony greeted them and set a rack of toast on the table.

"Fine old how-de-do in the galley," he told them. "The ice machine tipped over and there are ice cubes everywhere!"

41

Jay opened his mouth but Ann said quickly, "No, you *can't* go and look, Jay. I'm sure they've enough problems without nosy little boys pestering them."

"Sorry, sir," Tony agreed, "passengers aren't allowed in the galley."

When the meal was over, Jay wandered off towards the games room. It was a wonder, Ann thought, that he had not worn a groove in the floor along his well-trodden route. She went in search of Luke and found him alone in the card room studying the rules of backgammon. They exchanged accounts of the night and, as Ann had suspected, Luke and Sven had been very uncomfortable. As a result, Sven felt ill and Luke had persuaded him to stay in bed.

"I called the doctor," he told Ann "but so many other people want him Sven just has to wait his turn. I just hope it is seasickness and nothing worse." He looked worried.

"But surely – " said Ann. "Sven is so fit."

"But he is nearly seventy," Luke reminded her. "I offered to stay with him but he hates to be fussed over. I'll check back from time to time to see if he needs anything."

They made their way unsteadily towards the notice board.

Luke peered over her shoulder. "What's on this morning? A lecture on Dickens. No thanks! Or there's a talk on 'Colour Schemes in the Home'. No, I think I'll go for a swim instead."

"No such luck," Ann told him. "In bad weather they have to drain the pools otherwise the water splashes all over the place."

His face fell. "I hadn't thought of that. Then it's the library – they've got some good magazines – and then at ten thirty I'll nip back and see how Sven is."

Ann decided to learn about colour schemes so she made her way to the theatre where two young ladies were setting up exhibition stands on the stage. On either side of this two long velvet curtains hung full length and these swayed with the movement of the ship. There were ten minutes before the talk was due to start and Ann began thinking about Sven and hoping that his illness would not prove too serious.

A few people drifted in but obviously many more who would have attended were not feeling well enough to do so.

Suddenly she caught sight of a familiar figure several rows ahead of her. It was Hettie Bell, making her way along to a seat near the centre gangway. Impulsively, Ann left her own seat and hurried down to join her. By the time she arrived Mrs Bell had opened her handbag and was taking out a chequebook and pen.

"Good morning, Mrs Bell," said Ann. "How

are you feeling today? Is your head better?" Mrs Bell gave her a puzzled look.

"My head? What do you mean, dear?"

"You had a pain in your head."

"A pain? No, dear. I don't think so."

"But you did!" Ann insisted. "You told me you had a bad pain and that a voice was— "

"Oh *that* pain," said Mrs Bell. "Yes, it's gone, dear, thank you. It went as soon as I remembered what I had to do. It was amazing really. Astonishing. The moment I realized what I had to do the pain went away. All I have to do is write the cheque. It's such a relief."

She unscrewed the cap of her fountain pen and closed her eyes in order to concentrate. "Now what was the name? It began with 'B'. I remember because I thought 'B' for Bell and I knew I'd remember that way."

The name beginning with "B"! That was exactly what Sven had been saying about Adam May. Suddenly all Ann's earlier suspicions returned. And why the chequebook? Ann had not a shred of evidence and yet she had the strongest feeling that Mrs Bell was about to become the victim of a trick of some kind. She felt as though pieces of a jigsaw were beginning to fall into place.

"Excuse me, Mrs Bell, but what are you writing?" she asked.

Mrs Bell smiled cheerfully. "Why, the cheque

44

of course. If only I'd realized earlier, I needn't have— "

"Why are you writing a cheque? Who is it for?"

Mrs Bell stared at her in surprise. "Really dear, I don't see that's any of your business," she said. "All I know is that I have to write it."

The pen began to move over the cheque.

"Mrs Bell! You mustn't!" said Ann. "Please! Don't sign anything. I can't explain but I'm sure you shouldn't write that cheque. Not just yet. Not unless you're certain about it. Just tell me who it's made out to."

"Certainly not!" Mrs Bell looked very annoyed. "I shall write a cheque whenever and to whoever I please."

Ann's mind was whirling. Mrs Bell had "heard a voice" telling her to write a cheque and yet she did not appear to know what she was doing or why. She had had a severe pain which only disappeared when she "remembered what she had to do". It was a weird story and it had a very false ring to it.

Ann steeled herself to ask again. "Who is that cheque made out to, Mrs Bell? Please tell me. I won't tell anyone else." As Ann leaned forward Mrs Bell's hand closed over the chequebook, shielding it.

"No one must know," she muttered. "No one." She scribbled furiously then tore the cheque out of her book, folded it twice and slipped it into her pocket. She then screwed the cap onto her pen and returned pen and chequebook to her handbag.

She smiled brightly at Ann. "I'm very interested in colour," she said as though their previous conversation had never taken place. "Last time I crossed I attended a lecture about the colours one should and should not wear. I'd been wearing a lot of grey, you know, and navy blue but they told me they aren't my best colours. Soft pastels suit me best – " She indicated her lavender outfit with a careless wave of her hand. "Pastels and white and gold. Because of my eyes. They're blue with gold flecks in them, you see. So I mustn't wear silver. Ah – I think they're going to begin."

There was nothing else to be said or done. Unwillingly, Ann went back a few rows and sat down. From where she sat she could at least keep an eye on Mrs Bell. She could not help wondering about the amount she had written on the cheque. And who was the mysterious man whose name began with "B"?

On the stage the taller of the two ladies introduced herself as Carolyn. "But do call me Carrie," she trilled. "All my friends do and I do hope that by the end of our little talk you will all look on us as friends."

Prim, short for Primrose, then introduced herself and the talk began. Ann tried to lose herself in the mysteries of matching fabrics, hidden contrasts, and complementary drapes but her mind was on other

46

things. Perhaps she should go to the captain and tell him her suspicions.

"A bed cover can reflect the main colour in a room," Carrie was saying, "or it can be used as a foil. By that I mean a contrast. A small amount of contrast will set off your main colour. Too much contrast will overwhelm it and ruin the effect. For instance, a room that is mainly, say, mushroom, can be lifted by touches of dark green. A cream background can come alive with a splash of red poppies on curtains or a dark blue stripe in the upholstery of a sofa."

On the far side of the theatre a door opened and Ann's throat contracted as she recognized the figure outlined against the lighted doorway. It was Adam May. He made straight for the centre aisle and bent his head to speak to Mrs Bell. At once she fumbled in her pocket and passed him something. Then, with a muttered apology to the ladies on the platform, Adam May left the theatre. As the door swung to behind him Ann knew she must act. The mysterious cheque had been for Adam May.

"I'm going to the captain," she told herself and marched out of the theatre before she could change her mind.

Five

Seeing the captain was not quite as easy as Ann had expected. The captain, it seemed, was always busy and usually made appearances only at dinner, and he dined of course in the Lucia Grill Room. Ann would have to have a very good reason for taking up his valuable time, but since she was not prepared to explain why she had to see him so urgently no one was particularly helpful. To Ann it seemed they were being deliberately *un*helpful and her fevered imagination began to hint at an elaborate conspiracy. Were *all* the ship's officers involved in the plot and determined to prevent her from exposing it? No, she told herself. That was absurd. But it took a long time to convince Chief Officer Williams that she had something to say to the captain which was of real importance.

At last the officer shrugged. "Well, I'll take you up to the bridge but I can't promise the captain will see you. If he says 'No' then 'No' it is and don't ask me again. I'm sticking my neck out for you as it is."

Ann tried to tell him how grateful she was but

he was already striding off and she had to hurry after him, clutching at various pieces of furniture to steady herself, for the ship continued to plunge and roll violently. Outside the door which led directly to the bridge she waited until the officer returned.

"He's not very pleased but he'll give you five minutes," he told her, "so I hope you've got something worth saying."

As Ann went through the door she was at once impressed by the size and complexity of the ship's control room. There were dials, switches, levers and wheels as well as a bewildering array of computer screens.

The captain stood waiting for her, his arms crossed over his chest. His expression was not exactly welcoming and Ann knew at once that he was not going to take her story seriously. However, she drew a deep breath and launched into a rapid account of all that had happened, finishing with her belief that something very sinister was taking place. To her surprise, he did not at once pour scorn on her story but stood silently, considering what she had said.

"So what *exactly* do you think is happening?" he asked at last. "It all sounds rather vague, to put it mildly."

Ann shook her head. "I think it's to do with extorting money from people," she told him, "but I can't quite see how it's being done."

"And the man at the centre of this supposed

intrigue is Mr Adam May? Is that what you think?"

"Yes. I'm sure Mrs Bell gave him a cheque."

"Maybe he runs some kind of charity," said the captain. "You can't just go around accusing people of fraud, you know."

Ann felt herself blushing. She never should have come, she told herself miserably. The attempt had been doomed to failure right from the start. Her instincts were to cut short the interview and make her escape but she bit her lip and determined to have one last try.

"Captain, I know it sounds crazy but I honestly do believe something crooked is going on and— "

"Miss Burnside," he interrupted her, "would you feel any happier if I showed you the letter I received from Hemmel and Wizeman? It is most irregular, of course, but if it will put an end to all this nonsense, I will willingly do so."

Ann hesitated. Would the letter prove anything, she wondered. But at least he was trying to help and it would be churlish to refuse.

"I'd like to see it," she told him. "Thank you."

To her surprise, he drew an envelope from his pocket and before she could stop herself she blurted out, "You're carrying it around with you?"

"The doctor told me of your visit," he said tersely. "We both had another look at the letter to satisfy ourselves that it was genuine."

Ann's spirits rose. So her visit had set the doctor

thinking and he must have had a few doubts or he would never have mentioned the matter to the captain. He opened the envelope and handed her the letter. Her eyes skimmed through it. It informed the captain that their firm was doing market research on a new anti-seasickness drug and asked his permission to send their agent, Mr Adam May, to advise the ship's doctor on the drug's proper administration. At the top of the paper there was the firm's logo, the letter H superimposed on the letter W. The scribbled signature at the bottom was indecipherable but the name was typed beneath it – A. N. Badmour.

Ann handed back the letter. "It's an unusual name," she said without much conviction.

The captain smiled coldly. "Please, Miss Burnside," he said, "do try to give in gracefully."

"I'm sorry," she said. "You're right, I suppose. Thank you for showing me the letter."

"Not at all. Now, if you'll excuse me – Oh, and Miss Burnside, don't bother my crew with any more of your wild notions. We really do have plenty to do just at present. We were forced two hundred miles off course to avoid the hurricane and now we are heading into a storm. We shall be at least seven hours late docking in New York."

"I understand," muttered Ann. "I'm sorry." And she left the bridge thoroughly chastened.

"Blast!" she whispered. Now presumably the story would do the rounds and the whole crew would be laughing at her behind her back – even Simon and Tony. It was a sobering thought but at least she had done her best. She had tried to warn them and if something terrible happened then no one could blame *her*.

"They can all jump in the lake!" she muttered. "They can all be swindled and hoodwinked and – and cheated by whatever and whoever. Why should I care? I shall spend the rest of the trip having an utterly selfish time, thinking of no one but myself and – Whoops!"

The ship gave a particularly nasty lurch and she lost her balance and clutched at a chair which promptly fell over so that she found herself sprawled on the floor.

A hand was extended to assist her and to her dismay she found herself looking up into the face of Adam May!

"Oh - er thank you," she muttered.

"This weather is most unfortunate," he said. "Let's hope nothing worse happens."

"Yes," said Ann, unable to meet his eyes. What did he mean by that last remark? Was it a warning? Or a threat? Had the doctor told him of her enquiries?

With a polite nod he helped her to her feet and then left her and she watched him go with mixed feelings. Then she drew a deep breath. She must stop these wild imaginings. She had seen the letter from Hemmel and Wizeman. Adam May was what he said he was.

She wondered where Luke was and decided to go along to his cabin to see if Sven was any better. She set off but halfway down the stairs she came upon Mrs Bell in a pitiable state. The old woman was sitting on the stairs clutching her stomach. Her face was ashen.

"I'm going to be sick," she moaned. "Help me someone. I'm going to be sick."

"No you won't!" said Ann as firmly as she could. "I'll help you back to your cabin, Mrs Bell, and then we'll call your steward." She reached out a hand but Mrs Bell shook her head.

"I can't," she said. "I daren't move. Oh, help me someone."

"I'm *trying* to help you!" cried Ann. "Grab hold of my hand. That's the way. Up you come – gently does it."

Somehow she coaxed Mrs Bell onto her feet and, after finding out the number of the cabin, took her to it. She helped her into the bathroom, then rang the stewardess and waited for her to appear.

It was impossible not to wonder just why Mrs Bell had paid five hundred dollars for a drug which was not working. Frowning with concentration Ann thought about the various other "wonder" drugs which had eventually proved to be dangerous or unstable in some way. Now, what was this one called? Remembering the slip of paper the doctor had given her, she retrieved it from her pocket and studied it.

"Anaphetabenzilene. Quite a mouthful," she said, then, grimaced at the unintended pun. Then her eye was taken by the top of the prescription pad. HATCHER AND WATERFORD. She stared at it for a moment.

"I knew I was going to be sick!" said Mrs Bell as she staggered out of the bathroom and flopped miserably onto her bed. "Where is that stewardess, for heaven's sake? Do ring again, dear."

Ann rang the bell. "Mrs Bell," she said. "I wonder why you are ill after spending all that money on the patch."

"All that money? Oh yes, ten thousand dollars. Oh well, dear, it's in a good cause, isn't it?"

"Ten thousand dollars!" gasped Ann. She was on the point of explaining that she was referring to the five hundred dollars for the patch when she changed her mind abruptly. Mrs Bell had given Mr May a cheque! Was it for ten thousand dollars?

"Was it in a good cause?" she asked.

"Yes dear, of course it was."

"What was it exactly?"

"Exactly? Oh, I don't know – but he did tell me. At least, somebody told me." She put a hand to her head. "Could you fetch me a glass of water, dear? I think I'll just sip it. It can't do any harm –

Oh, this wretched storm. I'll be glad when we reach New York."

Ann decided not to tell her that the ship would be late arriving. The poor woman had enough problems to cope with.

At that moment there was a knock on the door and the stewardess came in, a look of kindly concern on her face. Ann left Mrs Bell in her capable hands and made her way back along the corridor. Something was niggling at the back of her mind.

"Of course!" she cried suddenly. "The initials are the same. Hatcher Waterford and Hemmel and Wizeman!" Was that significant or merely a coincidence, she wondered. She was still pondering the question when she met up with Luke. One look at his face told her that all was not well.

"Fasten your seat belt!" he told her. "You aren't going to like this any more than I do."

"Aren't going to like what?"

"The doctor said there was nothing wrong with Sven except seasickness. He told him to rest and he'd send something along. Sven asked me to fetch him a library book and while I was gone – " He swallowed hard. "Well, when I got back he had a – "

Ann's eyes grew wide with alarm. "Oh no!"

"Yes," said Luke grimly. "He had a patch on his neck! He said Adam May had called in at the doctor's request. Of course, he doesn't know what we know so I didn't dare tell him. I didn't want to scare him so I tried to persuade him to let me take it off but he became almost paranoid about it. Started shouting. Refused point blank to let me near him. I gave up in the end and came to look for you. Where on earth have you been?"

Quickly Ann told him of her meeting with Mrs Bell in the theatre and her subsequent visit to the captain.

"Just when I'd made up my mind to give up the whole thing," she told him, "I met Mrs Bell again – and she *was* sick. So if the patch doesn't prevent seasickness, what does it do?" She glanced at her watch. "You realize we've missed lunch," she said.

"I'm not hungry," he told her. "I'm so worried about Sven. Suppose he starts hearing voices like Mrs Bell."

"He won't," said Ann. "Not Sven. He's so down-to-earth."

She suddenly remembered the coincidence of the two similar initials and explained them to Luke who listened with growing interest.

"I don't care what the captain says," he told her. "I think something smells. We must calm down and think logically about it. Let's get a sheet of notepaper and write it all down. That way it may become clearer."

"And it might not!" said Ann. "Still, let's give it a whirl. There's some notepaper in our cabin. Let's go there."

Six

They sat side by side on Ann's bed and stared at the sheet of paper in front of them.

Ann wrote "Number One" and then looked blankly at Luke. "Where do we start?" she asked.

"Number One – We think Adam May is an assumed name."

"Do we?"

"Yes," said Luke. "Sven remembered the man who Adam May resembles. His name was Bourn and he was involved in some kind of industrial espionage."

"A Russian spy, do you mean?"

"No, not that sort of espionage. This man Bourn was selling his firm's secrets to another firm and he was sent to prison."

Ann digested the information for a moment. "Does Sven think Mr May is Bourn?"

"No. Nothing so definite. Anyway, Bourn had a beard. Sven only said there was a resemblance."

Ann wrote, "Number One – Is May his real

name? Number Two – May resembles Bourn."
Then she looked up. "Number Three?"

Luke considered. "The wonder patch doesn't work."

She wrote again.

"And Number Four," he said "May's firm has the same initials as Hatcher Waterford."

When Ann had finished writing she said, "Sounds a bit thin, doesn't it?"

"Maybe but we haven't finished yet. Number Five is the cheque Mrs Bell wrote for ten thousand dollars— "

"And Number Six is the voice in her head."

In the middle of writing Number Six Ann paused. "I do wish Sven hadn't agreed to have the patch," she said. "If only we'd talked to him about our suspicions."

"So do I but at the time I didn't want to worry him. He was so happy with his 'keep fit' programme."

Ann finished her writing then said, "Maybe for Number Seven we could put the name on that letter which the captain received from Hemmel and Wizeman. I said it was an unusual name and he was so sarcastic. 'Do give in gracefully, Miss Burnside'! I wanted to crawl into a crack in the floorboards."

"Forget it," said Luke. "It was in a good cause. Even Sherlock Holmes had setbacks! What was the name?"

"It was A. N. Badmour. Does that sound unusual to you?"

He shrugged. "I don't think I've ever come across it before," he admitted. "Is that spelt M-O-O-R?"

"No. M-O-U-R."

He frowned. "It *is* rather odd. It sounds somehow contrived." His eyes lit up suddenly. "Hey! Write it down and see what it is backwards."

Ann did so. "Ruomdabna," she said with a giggle and then added, "Sorry. I think it's getting to me. But seriously, does Roumdabna mean anything? Could it be Russian or Finnish or something?"

"It could be but I wouldn't think so. After all, if May is Bourn, he's English, not Russian."

"So he was."

They both thought deeply for a while and then Ann said slowly, "Could it be a code? Each letter is the first letter of a word, maybe?"

Luke shook his head. "If it was in code and the letter was sent to the captain then he would have to know the code and that would mean he is in on the plot. We surely don't think he is. Not the captain."

"No, we don't," said Ann.

Luke scratched his head and continued to stare at the word. "It could be an anagram," he suggested.

"Well, it can't be an anagram of Adam May," said Ann, "because that's got two Ms in it and A.

59

N. Badmour has only got one. And there's no B in Adam May and no N and no— "

"Wait!" shouted Luke, almost leaping off the bed with excitement. "There's a B and an N in Bourn!"

Ann stared at him as her mind raced. "But what was Bourn's first name?"

His face fell. "Sven didn't say. Oh well, it was only an idea." He thought for a moment then his face brightened. "Let's work it backwards! Take Bourn away from A. N. Badmour and see what's left."

Ann's pen flew across the paper with feverish haste. "It leaves A-A-D-M," she said.

They looked at each other in triumph – the remaining letters rearranged spelled Adam!

"Adam Bourn!" whispered Ann. "Why, the cheeky so-and-so!" They looked at each other and their jubilation faltered as they realized the full implication of their discovery. They now knew beyond all reasonable doubt that Adam May was really Adam Bourn, an ex-convict, and the knowledge put them at terrible risk. No one else would believe them and it was just possible that Adam May had been told of their suspicions. If so, they would be up against an unscrupulous criminal with no one to turn to for help.

"I'm beginning to think," said Ann shakily, "that flying the Atlantic would have been safer after all!"

Luke was silent. He, too, was unnerved by their discovery. With an effort, he managed a crooked grin.

"Let's not panic," he said. "It's too late to turn back. Let's sort out the rest of our clues and see what we've got."

Ann pulled herself together with an effort. "O.K.," she said. "Let's concentrate on the initials on the notepaper."

"Yes, miss!" mocked Luke. "O.K. Let's go. If the drug does not stop seasickness then either Hemmel and Wizeman is a crooked firm or – " His eyes narrowed. "Or there is no such firm!"

"But the logo," said Ann. "I saw it on the letter heading that the captain showed me. It had H W in the corner – but wait! It didn't have the *whole* name which means . . . ?" She broke off. "What does it mean?"

"It means . . . " said Luke, thinking frantically, "it means – I've got it! Just call me a genius." It means that Bourn used to work for Hatcher and Waterford! He was sacked because he was selling their secrets – "

Ann went on. "But he already had some of their headed notepaper so to make it look as though he is now working for a reputable firm he invented the name Hemmel and Wizeman, and wrote to the captain on the H W notepaper. Luke. I'm scared!"

He put a comforting arm round her shoulders.

"I'm not feeling too good myself," he confessed. "I almost wish we didn't know."

Ann stared in silence at the sheet of paper in front of her. With a long shuddering sigh she continued. "So Bourn sends the captain a letter from a firm he's invented and meets the doctor and gains his confidence. Why? What is he aiming to do? And what on earth do the patches really do?"

Luke shrugged. "I wonder if Sven could remember what Bourn's original firm was developing. If he's not feeling too rough we could ask him."

Ann looked at him unhappily. "It seems awful bothering him when he's sick but I think it's important. Oh dear, why on earth did we have to be the people who stumbled on this? It's getting more and more hairy." She glanced down at the paper and gave a deep sigh.

Gently Luke took the paper from her and folded it up. "Look, put it away for now," he said. "I vote we give ourselves a break. Go to the gym or play cards. Anything to take our minds off it – just for half an hour."

Ann agreed willingly, only too pleased for the chance to try and forget the frightening revelations of the past twenty minutes.

She pushed paper and pen into the dressing table drawer and followed Luke out into the passage. Together they made their way up the stairs towards the first class accommodation. When they reached the cabin they met the steward coming out of Luke's stateroom.

"How is my stepfather?" Luke asked him.

The steward shook his head. "Running a bit of a fever, I'd say," he told them, steadying himself against the wall. "Rambling a bit. Can't make head or tail of it, I'm afraid. I did wonder whether to call the doctor but if it's just a bit of a fever I didn't want to bother him. He's got so many patients, what with the storm and everything. One old lady was thrown to the floor when the ship rolled and she fractured her collar bone. Poor old doc's rushed off his feet and now the nurse is feeling a bit groggy. I can't remember the last time we had a trip like this and that's the truth. Real unlucky we are, with the weather. I mean, some of the stewards are ill and that's almost unheard of. Oh! There's another bell ringing. I'm needed again. Excuse me."

They watched him go for a moment then exchanged worried looks.

"Let's go in," said Ann – although she understood Luke's reluctance to see his stepfather. The word "rambling" had filled them both with misgivings. Quietly they turned the door handle and went inside.

Sven lay flat on his back, staring up at the ceiling. With his hands he held the blanket under his chin and his lips moved continuously, sometimes wordlessly. At other times the words were painfully clear.

"Speak up, damn you," he muttered. "I can't hear what you're saying. You want what? I have to what? Don't hurt me! I'm trying – I'm trying to understand – " His eyes rolled suddenly, and he released the blankets and clutched his head with both hands. "Oh no! No! Is too much. It hurts. It hurts . . . "

"Sven!" cried Luke. "Look, it's me, Luke. Sven, listen. *Please!*"

Tentatively he took hold of the old man's arm but Sven resisted him and now both hands were clamped to his head. He groaned aloud then with an anguished cry rolled over in the bed to face the wall.

"I'm trying," he muttered, "but I can't understand. I can't hear you properly. Ah!"

Suddenly he released his head and lay motionless, but his breathing was rapid and shallow.

"Sven!" Luke tried again. "Hey there, it's me, Luke, come to see how you are. The steward said – "

He broke off as Sven's breathing suddenly changed again. This time to a deep steady rhythm.

"He's fallen asleep," said Luke. He tucked the covers around the old man's neck, and turned to Ann. "I guess I'd better stay with him. I don't like to leave him in this state."

Ann hesitated. "Luke," she said slowly. "Do you think you could possibly try to pull that wretched patch off while he's asleep?"

64

Luke looked doubtful. "I could try," he said, "but not right now. It's on the right side of his neck and that's the side he's lying on. Maybe later I'll have a go." He sighed. "What will you do?"

Ann straightened her shoulders. "I think I'll make a call on Mrs Bell," she said. "I'll come back later and report."

He looked at her anxiously. "Don't do anything I wouldn't do," he said.

"I won't," said Ann. "Don't worry about me. I'll be fine."

Seven

She found Mrs Bell in the lido at the stern of the ship. She was reclining in a lounger beside the small pool which had been emptied and covered with a net to prevent anyone from falling in. Mrs Bell's latest outfit was in shades of soft apricot. Ann saw, to her surprise, that she was no longer wearing the patch on her neck.

"Hi there!" cried Ann cheerfully settling in the next lounger. "How are you feeling?"

Mrs Bell put down the novel she was reading and smiled at Ann.

"Oh, I'm much better," she told her. "I'm a different woman. It's such a relief to feel well again and my appetite has returned, thank goodness. I've just ordered a pot of tea and a plate of fancy cakes. Perhaps you'd like to join me." Ann accepted and when the stewardess arrived a second cup and saucer was requested and speedily brought. While Ann munched her way through a chocolate eclair she let Mrs Bell chatter on, waiting for a chance to slip in a few questions.

"I do so love this ship!" Mrs Bell enthused. "Every little whim is catered for and you get the feeling they *care* about you. Do you feel that, dear?" Ann said she did.

"And the food – well, what can I say?" Mrs Bell went on. "Breakfast, bouillon at eleven – that's soup you know, dear – then lunch and now a teatime snack. Though my late husband teased, he used to encourage me to eat, you see, and it's become a habit. Poor Edgar. He did so hate skinny women. He used to call me 'his armful'. Wasn't that cute?"

Ann said it was. Mrs Bell began a second cream slice and Ann took her chance.

"A friend of mine has gone down with seasickness and he's bought one of those patches."

Mrs Bell paused in the demolition of the cream slice and her hand strayed to her neck.

"Oh that," she said. "I've taken it off now." She glanced round her and lowered her voice. "To be perfectly honest dear, it didn't seem to do much good. I still felt very sick. In the end Mr May told me to take it off. Said it didn't suit me. The steward gave me two little white pills and they did the trick. I could have saved myself five hundred dollars but never mind. I feel well again. So, if you get sick, dear, just ask your cabin steward. They probably all have those little white tablets."

She finished off the slice and delicately licked

cream from her podgy fingers. "I just adore cream cakes," she said.

Ann took a deep breath. "My friend," she said. "He's hearing the same voice that you heard."

"Voice?" echoed Mrs Bell. "What voice, dear?"

"The one telling you to do something," she said. "It's telling him to do something but he can't quite hear what."

Mrs Bell stared at her. "What on earth are you talking about?" she demanded. "I didn't hear any voice."

"The voice that told you to write a cheque," said Ann.

"Write a cheque?" The old lady looked completely baffled.

"Yes." Ann met her eyes steadily. "The voice told you to write a cheque for ten thousand dollars and give it to Mr May."

Mrs Bell blinked. "Are you mad?" she asked. "Why should I give Mr May ten thousand dollars? I hardly know the man."

"But I *saw* you give it to him," said Ann. "In the theatre during the talk on Colour Schemes in the Home."

Mrs Bell shook her head. "I'm sorry, dear," she said calmly. "You're mixing me up with someone else. I have never given Mr May a cheque for ten thousand dollars and I didn't go to that talk."

"But I saw you there – " Ann began.

"Another cup of tea, dear?"

"Er- no thank you."

Mrs Bell refilled her own cup then smiled at Ann. "I do hope your friend will soon be better. It really can't be very pleasant to hear voices. I should tell the doctor if I were you, dear. He may be delirious. Poor Edgar was delirious once but he had influenza."

Ann made one last effort. "Mrs Bell, could I ask you a favour?" she asked. "I know it won't make sense to you but would you take a look at your chequebook and make sure you didn't write that cheque. I know it sounds stupid but it might help me. I'm a bit confused at present."

"You certainly are, dear," said Mrs Bell somewhat testily, "but if it makes you feel any better, I will." With a shrug of her plump shoulders, she reached for her straw handbag and rummaged inside.

"Ah, here we are!" she cried. "Now let me see." She flicked carefully through the cheque stubs, muttering to herself as she did so.

"There's the $500 for the patch," she said. "And that's the last one – Oh no, wait a minute. What's this?"

Ann hardly dared breathe. Was this the proof they had been waiting for?

Mrs Bell frowned. "That's odd," she said. "There's a cheque missing and nothing on the stub. Oh, that is downright careless of me. Now whatever could that have been?"

"It could have been for ten thousand dollars," said Ann dejectedly. "I should have known. He's much cleverer than I thought and I thought he was pretty clever."

"Edgar always used to grumble at me for doing that. 'You've got to write on the stubs, Hettie,' he used to say." She brightened. "Ah! Wait now. perhaps it was the hairdresser – " She patted her hair but then shook her head. "No, that can't be it. That's tomorrow at ten thirty. At least I think so." She found a small blue diary and flicked through the pages. "Yes, ten thirty tomorrow. Now what could it have been, I wonder, if it wasn't the hairdresser? Oh well, it will come back to me in time. Shall I tell you if it does? Would that settle your mind, dear?"

"Yes, please," said Ann and nearly added, "but it won't come back to you."

She made her excuses and left the lido. At least she had learned a little more, she consoled herself. She knew that after the unfortunate victims had parted with their money the whole episode was erased from their memory. She would have to warn Luke or Sven might be robbed in the same way. But first things first. She would make a quick trip to the games room to see that Jay was all right.

The children's games room was situated at the top of a narrow flight of stairs and it was supervised by a charming young woman whom Ann recognized from their last crossing as Sarah Williams. The room was full of computers and video games, all clicking and whirring. The noise was deafening as children of all ages urged on the heroes of their games or shouted excitedly to each other. She wondered how Sarah could stand the perpetual clamour. Jay was nowhere to be seen so she asked Sarah if she had seen him.

"Oh yes, he was here," Sarah told Ann, "until about half an hour ago. Then a gentleman came to fetch him." Ann stared at her and her heart contracted with sudden fear.

"A – a gentleman?" she stammered. "Not Mr May!"

"He didn't give his name."

"Tall?" said Ann, while a tight knot of anxiety formed inside her. "Maybe in his forties? A bit sinister looking really, with strange eyes?"

Sarah shook her head. "No, he was plumpish and about thirty I'd say. American accent. He had a little girl with him. He called her Emma, I remember. She'd taken quite a fancy to your brother, by all accounts. I think they were heading for the shops."

Ann breathed a sigh of relief. "Thank you," she said, "I'll look there first."

The thought of Jay with an admirer amused Ann as she made her way to the wide curving staircase that led up from the Queen's Room to the gallery of shops above.

Sure enough she found Jay with a pleasant-faced man and a girl a little older than Jay. Her brother seemed quite at ease in the company of his new friends.

Ann introduced herself and the man told her his name was Alan Kaufman and that Emma was his only child.

"I can't believe it," said Ann. "Someone has actually managed to lure Jay away from the video games. Your daughter must have great charm."

Alan smiled fondly at his daughter. "Well, I guess I'm prejudiced but I think the world of her. It's her tenth birthday today and I asked her what she would most like. You know what she said? To buy something nice for Jay! She met him yesterday in the games room and quite fell for him!"

Jay held up a dark blue leather wallet stamped in silver with a picture of the *Santa Lucia*. "It's a present from Emma," he told her. "I shall keep all my money in it."

"What, *all* of it?" teased Alan. "If you're going to be a millionaire – "

Jay grinned. "I said I was going to invent a new video game and Alan said that if I did I'd probably make a fortune."

"Well, here's hoping," said Ann. "The sooner the better."

Jay looked at Emma. "I've already got a good idea for one," he told her. "Let's go and find some paper and I'll sketch it out for you."

They went off cheerfully together and Alan laughed. "What he really means is that we're cramping his style."

He was, as Sarah had said, in his early thirties but looked very boyish with crinkly ginger hair, blue eyes and rather a lot of freckles. He suggested that they find somewhere to sit down as the movement of the ship was still considerable, making it tiring to stand. They settled themselves at a table for two in the gallery and Ann asked casually about the rest of his family.

"There's no one else," he told her. "My wife and son are both dead but I don't want to bore you with – "

Ann said quickly, "Maybe you'd rather not talk about it."

"Oh, don't worry on that score," he said grimly. "I'm used to talking about it. I've been doing nothing else for the last few years. It's over now, thank goodness, but – " He broke off. "I'm sorry. I'm not making any sense. If you're sure you won't be bored, I'll start at the beginning."

"Please do," said Ann, wondering what to expect. The story began when his wife, Liza, had their second child, a little boy named Andrew. "He was a beautiful bouncing boy," said Alan, "and for three

73

weeks he made excellent progress, putting on weight – all that stuff. Then one morning we woke up and he was dead in his cot."

"Oh no!" whispered Ann, shocked.

He nodded. "There was no reason for it – the doctors called it a cot death. Apparently it's quite common. The doctors are trying to find out what goes wrong." He sighed. "It hit us both hard, of course, but Liza kept blaming herself. She became very depressed until she couldn't cope with Emma and her mother came to help out. She got steadily worse and finally she had to go into hospital for treatment. While she was in there she was given a very new drug – without my permission – and it killed her."

Ann was horrified. "But that's illegal, isn't it?"

He nodded again. "The hospital tried to hush everything up, but I'm a journalist and I made up my mind to fight them. I wanted to get the truth into the open before someone else died."

Ann smiled faintly. "So they took on more than they bargained for."

"They certainly did! My editor told me to go ahead and I enlisted the help of colleagues on other newspapers in other areas. Between us we tracked down another four similar cases. One in Boston, one in Redding, California, one in Tucson, Arizona and the last in New York. I was going to sue the hospital but my lawyer told me it would be

74

more effective to sue the company that made the drug."

"What sort of drug was it?" Ann asked.

"You may well ask!" he said grimly. "It took months of probing before we found out. It was a highly secret mind-control drug – the sort of thing you read about in spy novels. The mind of the person who takes it can be manipulated by the person who administers it."

"Like hypnotizing someone?"

"Exactly, and afterwards they would remember nothing."

"But why use that on your wife? She wasn't a spy."

"No, she wasn't, but they wanted to control her mind while they convinced her that she was in no way responsible for the death of our son. If the drug had been properly tested it could have been most beneficial – a medical and scientific breakthrough. The trouble was it *hadn't* been properly tested and they got the dosage wrong. They gave her too much of it. And she died."

"What a terrible story," said Ann. "What happened, then, when you took them to court?"

"I won – or rather *we* won. We fought the case for all five victims. They finally admitted liability. We won compensation and the company was heavily fined. They had to blame someone so they made a scapegoat out of one of their best scientists – a man named Adam Bourn. They didn't— "

"Adam Bourn!" gasped Ann. She stared at him. "Adam Bourn as in Hemmel and Wizeman?"

"Never heard of them," said Alan. "The drug company was called Hatcher and Waterford. This Bourn was a very clever man. They didn't sack him because he was too valuable to them. They moved him to another department but the scandal ruined his reputation. So he took his revenge by selling some of the company's secrets to a rival firm and for *that* he went to prison."

Ann was shaking her head in disbelief. Here at last was someone who would believe her own story!

Alan was looking at her curiously. "What do you know about Adam Bourn then?" he asked. "I thought I knew all there was to know about that man."

"Oh, but you *don't*, Alan," Ann told him, her eyes gleaming with excitement. "Settle yourself comfortably and I will tell you *my* story. I think you'll find it very interesting! Adam Bourn is on board this ship."

Eight

Ann told him all that had happened so far and Alan's eyes did not leave her face until she had finished.

Then he said slowly. "So, he's out of prison. He thinks society owes him something and this is his way of getting it. Do you see what he's doing?"

"I think so," said Ann. "Using what I already knew and adding what you've told me, I can put two and two together."

She frowned in concentration. "Let me see if I've got it right. Adam Bourn comes out of prison with nothing. No money, no job – and no chance of a job after all the bad publicity. He has to rely on his wits plus the knowledge he has about the mind control drug. Am I right so far?"

Alan nodded and she went on. "He thinks of a way to get money out of very rich people. He sells the idea of the anti-seasickness patch to the captain of the *Santa Lucia*— "

"And no doubt he plans to move on to other luxury cruise ships," said Alan.

She nodded. "An unlimited source of income! Very clever."

"Oh, he's clever. No doubt about that."

She went on. "Once a victim is wearing the patch he is told to write a cheque made out to Bourn and when they've done it he collects it and leaves them alone. The drug wears off and they have no recollection of what's happened. No memory of it and a blank cheque stub in the chequebook. It's ingenious."

"Your friend Sven – you must make sure he doesn't part with any money."

"He's safe for the time being," said Ann, "because Luke's sitting with him. Luke will be over the moon when he hears we have an ally at last! It's such a relief to find someone who doesn't think we're mad!"

Alan smiled. "I *know* you're not mad," he said. "What I don't know for sure is what to do next."

"What *I* don't understand is how Bourn hasn't recognized you from the court case."

"He hasn't seen me," said Alan. "I've been locked away in my cabin working. I'm writing a book about the whole sorry business and I want to get it finished before I get back to New York. I only emerged because it was Emma's birthday."

Ann was thinking hard. "So Bourn doesn't know you're on board. What do you think will happen if he finds out?"

"I don't know but he'll almost certainly stop what he's doing – and we shall have the devil's own job to prove anything."

"Unless we find the cheques!"

They looked at each other like two conspirators. Ann said, "I shouldn't fancy trying to search his room."

"*I* would!" said Alan. "But we'd need a diversion. Something that would keep his attention elsewhere while I slip into his cabin."

"Slip in?" cried Ann. "How can you? You don't have a key."

He tapped the side of his nose with a knowing smile. "There are ways and means," he told her.

Ann looked at him apprehensively. Suddenly she felt that the whole affair was moving into another league. It was beginning to sound distinctly dangerous.

"But if you get caught in his room *you'll* be in trouble," she suggested.

"He's not going to catch me," Alan assured her.

Ann nodded but she still felt uneasy. She and Luke had been reasonably cautious and level-headed but there was a certain gleam in Alan's eyes which made her nervous. Sighing deeply, she decided it was too late now. She had confided in him and she hoped Luke would approve. Perhaps any ally was better than none.

"I think I'd better go and see Luke," she said,

"and tell him what's new. Will you be here when I get back?"

"Probably."

"I won't be long then – Oh, and by the way. Bourn now has no beard so he'll look different."

"I'll look exactly the same to him," said Alan, a trifle bitterly, "only much older. But don't worry, I'll bury my face in a book if I see him coming."

Ann turned to go but a sudden terrible thought struck her.

"Alan!" she gasped. "The passenger list! He's read it. He'll *know* you're on board."

To her surprise he grinned. "No, he won't," he told her. "As a journalist I write under the name of Alan Brent, that's my mother's maiden name. He won't recognize the name Kaufman which is my real name."

She breathed a sigh of relief and went off to find Luke.

She tapped on the door and Luke opened it, looking flushed and upset.

"Luke, what's wrong?" she said. "Is it Sven? Is he worse?"

Luke shook his head dejectedly. "Not in the way you mean," he told her. "He's not having pains in his head any more and he's not rambling."

"He's not? Then what's the matter? I don't get it."

"He's not as rich as he was."

It took a moment or two for the meaning of his words to sink in.

"Luke no!" she gasped. "You mean he's written a cheque for Bourn? But how could he? You've been with him all the time."

Luke's eyes smouldered angrily. "Not *all* the time," he corrected. "I was here until half an hour ago when the steward came to the door. Said I was to go to the Purser's Office to collect a message for Sven. I didn't suspect a thing. I locked the door behind me and went off. It's quite a way and when I got there there was a queue so I had to wait. When it was my turn they didn't know anything about a message. Said it was obviously a mistake and apologized. I guessed at once that it was our friend Bourn up to his tricks so I ran like mad all the way back. Sven was alone, breathing more evenly."

"Was the door still locked?"

"Oh yes. The wretched man had been very efficient. I went straight to the drawer of the dressing table where Sven keeps his wallet and chequebook. Look for yourself." He opened the drawer, took out a chequebook and handed it to Ann. Slowly, she turned the pages and found what she expected. The last cheque stub was blank! They looked at each other in dismay.

"So the steward is in on the plot," she said.

"Not necessarily. And I doubt it. It would be rather risky for Bourn to let anyone else in on what he was doing. Also, if the steward knew he could always blackmail Bourn. Demand money in exchange for keeping quiet. I don't think Bourn would take risks of that sort. My guess is he's working alone. Bourn phoned the steward and pretended to be the purser. I keep wondering how much the cheque was for."

"Couldn't Sven stop the cheque? Couldn't he write to his bank – or telephone them?"

"He could if he thought it was necessary," said Luke, "but when the drug wears off he won't remember anything about it. It may be days before the effects finally wear off. By the time I can convince him it will be too late. You can bet Bourn will cash the cheques the moment he lands in New York."

Ann sat down thoughtfully in the armchair. "Couldn't *you* phone the bank and explain the situation?"

He gave a short laugh. "You think they'd believe me? I feel so angry with myself," he exploded suddenly. "I should have guessed it was a trick."

"I don't see how," said Ann. "I would have been taken in by it. Collecting a message sounds reasonable. You're being too hard on yourself, Luke. We're up against a very clever man."

"But what am I to do? I can't bear to think of Sven being robbed. He's worked hard all his life for that money and now that awful Bourn – " He shook his head dejectedly.

"We have to concentrate on getting the cheques back," said Ann, "and I've got news for you."

She launched into an account of her meeting with Alan and was pleased to see that the prospect of an ally dispelled a little of Luke's gloom.

"I'll go back now and tell him what's happened here," she concluded. "Maybe you could come too. After all, Bourn's not likely to bother Sven again. He's got the cheque which is what he wants and remember – he doesn't know how much *we* know. He probably doesn't think that you know about the cheque Sven has given him."

"Unless the captain told him what you suspected," Luke replied. "Just to be on the safe side we'll assume that he knows quite a lot. Then we shan't underestimate him. But you're right about one thing. He's not going to come back now he's got the cheque. I'll come with you for half an hour or so. I'd like to meet Alan Kaufman. He sounds like a useful person to know."

Carefully locking the door behind them, they hurried to rejoin Alan. Ann quickly made the introductions.

Luke then told him of the latest development and Alan looked thoughtful.

"So now we know Bourn has a duplicate key to your cabin," he told Luke. "That means he may have a complete set of keys – or just duplicates for the doors of the people he intends to rob.

That seems more logical with hundreds of passengers on board. I wonder how he got them." He grinned at Ann and Luke. "I think it's time for me to have a look round *his* cabin," he said calmly.

"But how?" they said together. Ann went on, "Do *you* have duplicate keys?"

"No," he said, "but I have a little 'know-how'. Don't fuss, I won't get caught."

"But you might," said Luke, looking distinctly worried. "If he comes back and catches you in there— "

"He won't," Alan told them, "because we shall catch him the way he caught you."

Ann looked doubtful. "With a bogus message, you mean? But then when he finds the cheques gone and realizes he's been tricked he'll guess— "

"Oh, but I shan't take them," said Alan. "I want him to be caught with the evidence. No point in me presenting the cheques to the captain. Bourn could deny all knowledge of them. No, for the moment we've got to let him keep them. All I want to do is find out where they are."

For a moment they were all silent, considering how best to keep Bourn busy so that Alan could take a look inside his cabin.

"It's no good," said Ann at last, "I don't like the idea of the bogus message. It gives so much away. Bourn will know for sure that someone is suspicious

84

of him. I vote we try to think of some other way to keep him out of the way."

"Such as?" said Alan.

"I don't know yet. I'm thinking."

Luke said, "I agree with Ann. So far we have an ace up our sleeve – Bourn doesn't know that Alan is on board. Now, he must know that Ann and I wouldn't break into his cabin so if he guesses the reason for the bogus message he might also guess that someone else, an *adult*, has joined forces with us."

Alan nodded reluctantly. "You're right," he said. "Good thinking. We'll try and come up with something else."

"What about dinner time?" Ann suggested suddenly. "If he comes in to dinner I'll know because he sits at our table. Where do you eat, Alan?"

"Oh, the *Santa Lucia* restaurant," he said. "I'm travelling transatlantic class, like you."

After some discussion, they agreed a plan which would be put into operation if Bourn decided to go into dinner. Jay would be invited to sit at Alan's table to share Emma's special birthday cake which the stewards had promised to provide as a surprise for her. The moment Bourn joined Ann and the others at the table she would ask Simon or Tony to take a message to Alan's table. Alan would at once leave the restaurant and could expect to be undisturbed for at least thirty minutes while Bourn

85

ate his meal. The only problem was that the sea was still rough and Bourn might not feel well enough to eat. They would have to wait and see. Ann smiled at her fellow conspirators and crossed her fingers for luck.

"It's O.K. for you two," grumbled Luke, "but I shall be stuck away in the first class restaurant. I shan't know what's happening."

"Don't worry," said Ann. "We'll meet you as soon as the meal's over and tell you everything."

That evening Ann went in to dinner without Jay and sat down at their table, which was empty. A few other diners were groping their way towards their tables and the stewards hurried to and from the galley with precariously balanced trays. Through the huge windows Ann could see mountainous grey waves rolling past as the ship ploughed forward. She had never seen such angry seas and was grateful for the fact that she was on such a large ship. Simon appeared at her side with his usual welcoming smile and handed her the menu.

"Is Modom dining alone?" he asked. "Where's young master Jay?"

"He's been invited to a birthday party."

"And you're not invited?"

"I'm rather old," she laughed. "Oh, here comes Mabel Hubbard. That's nice. She must be feeling better."

Mabel sank thankfully into her chair. "Now I know what an earthquake feels like!" she joked. "The floor keeps moving and the walls won't stay put."

She accepted her menu and they both greeted Tony who brought the bread rolls.

"Nice to see you again," he told Mabel. "Feeling better, I hope?"

"Oh yes, much better, thank you."

At that moment a tall figure loomed behind Tony and Ann's heart missed a beat as she recognized Bourn.

"Ah, Mr May," said Tony. "How are you surviving today?"

He grunted something inaudible, took a brown bread roll and helped himself to butter.

Ann made a mental note. She must not let the name Bourn slip out inadvertently.

"Good evening, Mr May," she said brightly.

He glanced at her coldly without replying and ordered mock turtle soup followed by steak and broccoli.

Ann turned to Tony. "Would you be kind enough to take a message to Emma Kaufman," she said. "Just say 'Happy Birthday' from Ann. She's at one of the tables on the far side of the restaurant. Jay is with her."

"Certainly," he said and hurried away across the room. For a minute or two Ann did not dare glance round but when she did she saw that Alan had gone from his table.

Mabel began to chatter about her husband who had fallen and hurt his ankle. She explained that although it was only a sprain, he had thought it safer not to venture too far until the sea was calmer. Alice was staying with him and they would eat in their cabin. Ann nodded from time to time but her thoughts were with Alan and she prayed that he would get in and out of Bourn's cabin undetected. After what seemed like an eternity, but was in fact just less than twenty minutes, she saw him take his place once more. Catching her eye he shook his head slightly and her heart sank. He had not found the cheques.

Just as the main course was being served, the ship hit a big wave and they were all jolted half out of their seats. Wine glasses tipped over and several of the stewards lost their balance and fell, taking their trays with them to the floor.

Mabel laughed nervously. "Oh dear," she said. "It really is quite frightening. I try not to look at the windows. One minute the sky disappears and we seem to be under the water, then we roll the other way and there's nothing but sky. It really will be marvellous to set foot on dry land again."

"We'll probably roll about like drunken sailors when we do," said Ann. "We'll be so used to compensating for the ship's roll."

Ann kept thinking about the cheques. They must be on Bourn's person – unless, perhaps, they were locked for safe keeping in the Purser's Office safe. If only she had x-ray eyes, she thought. The cheques could be very near her, in his wallet, most probably in an inside pocket. She wanted to scream with frustration.

At that moment, however, Fate took a hand. Without any warning another freak wave hit the ship which gave a terrifying lurch. This time tables tilted crazily and plates of food slid to the floor. Chairs tipped over, some backwards, some sideways and there were screams of alarm as the diners were thrown to the floor amid spilt food and broken crockery. Within seconds the elegant restaurant was a shambles. From a table nearby a groan went up followed by a quavering voice. "My arm! I think it's broken!"

Fallen stewards scrambled to their feet and rushed at once to help the passengers. Ann had been thrown sideways from her chair but she was not hurt and quickly picked herself up. She turned to Mabel who was badly shaken and had a small cut on her forehead.

"Oh Ann!" she gasped. "Oh, isn't this dreadful. For a terrible moment I thought we were going to sink. I thought – we've hit an iceberg like the Titanic and we're all going to be drowned. I know it's silly but these things do happen." She put a trembling hand to her forehead. "Oh, I'm bleeding!"

"It's only a small cut," Ann reassured her as she helped her to sit up. "I expect it was a broken plate or something."

"I'll just stay here on the floor," said Mabel, "while I pull myself together. You look after poor Mr May."

Ann turned in surprise and found him stretched unconscious on the floor, his right elbow in a mess of broccoli. She saw also that his jacket had fallen open. There, in full view, was the top edge of his wallet!

Without stopping to think she snatched the wallet from his pocket. With frantic haste she riffled through it, and found several cheques. She reclosed the wallet and thrust it back into May's pocket. Her heart was beating so fast she could hardly breathe and felt as though she was suffocating. It had all taken no more than a few seconds.

Then Tony was kneeling beside her, loosening Bourn's tie, an anxious look on his face.

"What a to-do," he said.

Ann forced a faint smile. "A 'to-do' you call it? That must be the understatement of the year!" she said.

Bourn's eyes flickered open. "What happened?" he asked dazedly.

Tony said, "You were thrown from your chair

sir, when we hit that massive wave. I think you probably hit your head on the serving bay."

Bourn put up a hand to his head but then changed his mind and quickly felt inside his jacket for his wallet.

Ann felt herself go hot and cold. If he had opened his eyes just a few seconds earlier, he would have seen her with the wallet. Whatever had induced her to take such a terrible risk? She felt weak at the knees. Still, she had seen the cheques. One signed by Hettie Bell, another by Sven. They had proof at last.

Nine

Fifteen minutes later a degree of order had been restored to the dining room. The injured had been taken to the ship's hospital and the worst of the mess on the carpet had been cleaned up. The tables had been relaid and fresh food produced and served.

Bourn was no longer with them so Mabel and Ann sat together enjoying the rest of their meal.

Ann had taken the opportunity to visit Alan's table to see that Jay was all right but two other people were sharing the table with them so she could say nothing to Alan about her discovery of the cheques.

They all met up later, however, in Ann's cabin while Jay and Emma played draughts in the card room. Ann told them about the cheques and Alan congratulated her on her initiative. Luke looked worried.

"You could have been accused of stealing," he pointed out. "If he had seen you with the wallet it would have looked very bad."

Alan agreed that it was a rash thing to do but

added, "Still, I'm not saying I'm sorry you did it but perhaps in future you'd better leave the heroics to me." He leaned forward. "Obviously, I didn't find the cheques in his cabin but I *did* find several things of interest. A beretta, would you believe?"

Luke whistled in amazement but Ann looked blank.

"A *gun*," Luke told her.

"Christopher!" she said faintly.

Alan nodded. "It was in the bottom of his wardrobe, pushed into one of his shoes. Now we know the sort of man we're up against. He's pretty ruthless. That's why I don't want you two taking any more risks. The other thing I found was a case containing a hypodermic syringe and several small phials containing a clear liquid."

Ann said. "So, is he a drug addict as well as a crook?"

"Not necessarily," said Alan. "I have to admit that I don't know a lot about drugs – and I don't *want* to – but my instinct tells me it wasn't that sort of drug. I can't explain it but it was a professional looking case, the sort of thing a doctor might carry. I just don't know."

"Well," said Ann after a brief silence. "What's the next step?"

"I was thinking over dinner," said Luke. "Why doesn't Alan ask the ship's doctor to have one of the patches analysed? They might listen to him. Then they'll know that it's a mind-control drug. They won't need to take our word for it."

Alan shook his head. "It would take too long," he objected. "They would have to send it to a laboratory when we reach New York and by that time Bourn would be gone and the money too. We'd never be able to convince all his victims that they had been robbed. By the time the findings of the lab report were made known, the cheques would be cleared and Bourn would be away, living it up in South America."

"You're right," Luke sighed. "Somehow we have to bring matters to a head before we dock."

"Wait a minute," said Ann. "Let's get out the list we made earlier and go through it. It might help to refresh our minds and we can also add the new information such as the beretta and – " She began to rummage in the drawer but suddenly said, "Oh no!"

"What's up?" asked Alan.

"The sheet of paper – the list – it's gone!"

Luke gave a gasp of dismay. "Bourn?"

"Could be."

"Then he *knows* we know."

"I hope not," said Alan, his expression serious. "Have another look, Ann. You may be mistaken."

Desperately, she pulled out the drawer and together they searched for the missing paper. It was as she had feared. The incriminating list had gone.

"Maybe Jay has taken it," Luke said without much hope.

"Why should he?" Ann countered. "He could never read my scribble – he never can – so it would be meaningless to him. I just *know* it was Bourn. Fancy him being in here – Ugh! It gives me the creeps."

She covered her face with her hands and Luke put a comforting arm round her shoulders.

"It's my fault," she whispered. "I should have torn it up."

Alan shook his head. "There's no need to panic. We must keep our heads. If he's taken it, it's because he wants you to know that he's on to you. He wants to scare you."

"He *has* scared me!" said Ann shakily. She was grateful for Luke's arm round her shoulders.

Luke said. "O.K. so he knows – but even if he knows, what can he do to us?"

"Shoot us!" said Ann. "With the beretta. That would be a *very* good way to scare us."

Alan said. "He'd never dare. Remember, he doesn't think you have any real proof and he doesn't know I'm in on it. So we do have a surprise or two up our sleeves."

"I've been wondering," said Alan, when they had all met up again later next day. "Suppose I go to Bourn's cabin with a hidden tape recorder and tell

95

him who I am and what we know about him. If I'm lucky he might agree that what I say is true but challenge me to prove it. I then say I can't but I'll have a damn good try and he'll think he's called my bluff. Then we take the tape to the captain."

"A tape recorder!" said Ann. "Of course."

"It's a pocket-sized version but adequate. I could carry it in my jacket pocket. It doesn't whirr or anything. He'd never know."

Luke and Ann exchanged looks.

"Too risky," said Ann. "Suppose he just shoots you?"

"He'd have to get rid of my body."

"Dump it over the side," said Luke.

Ann shook her head despairingly. "Stop! This is crazy!" she cried. "Shooting people and dumping them in the sea. It sounds like a nightmare." She looked at the others. "It *is* a nightmare – only it's daylight and I'm wide awake!"

Alan glanced at the watch on his wrist and said. "Damn! It's nearly time for the talent show and I've promised Emma she can watch it. Are you two going?"

"Talent show?" groaned Ann. "I'd forgotten all about it. I'll have to because Jay always takes part. He sings 'The Teddy Bears Picnic' and everyone gives him a tremendous round of applause because he's usually one of the youngest performers. He collects the medals. He's got dozens."

"Medals?" Luke looked baffled.

Ann smiled. "They're medallions really – a memento to prove that you took part in the show on board the *Santa Lucia*. You can't get the medallions any other way." She sighed. "If we all go we'd better not sit together in case Bourn sees us."

Alan said. "I doubt if he watches talent shows."

"Probably not," said Ann, "but it's held in the Queen's Room and he could easily look down from the gallery above."

"But the children will want to be together," said Alan. "I think I'll stay away. Maybe have a drink in the bar or watch the gambling in the casino. I'll do some hard thinking and maybe come up with an idea."

Luke thought he ought to stay with Sven and decided to eat his dinner in their cabin. It was agreed that Ann would go to the show with the two children so that everything would appear as normal as possible and Bourn would not know whether or not they had discovered that the list was missing.

The talent show was due to start at seven o'clock and end at seven forty five so that no one had to miss their evening meal.

At one minute past seven Bob Stuart, the entertainments manager, stepped onto the centre of the floor, picked up the microphone and bowed in all directions. He was young and plump and full of fun.

"Good evening, ladies and gentlemen," he boomed cheerfully. "Tonight is the night we've all been waiting for, when you, the passengers, entertain us. You'll be pleased to know that as usual on these occasions, we have a splendid and varied programme. Now, before we start, I'd just like to remind you that it takes a lot of guts for our performers to stand out here and entertain you, so let's show each and every one that we really do appreciate them." He glanced over his shoulder. "Ah, I see that our first act is ready and waiting." He consulted his clipboard. "It's Sue Bridger from Glasgow and she's going to sing for you. Let's give her a big hand!"

Applause broke out as Miss Bridger appeared in a turquoise blue evening dress. Behind her, the three-piece band struck up a few bars of "Loch Lomond" and she began to sing. On Ann's right Jay began to fidget. Emma sat next to him.

"I'm third," he whispered loudly. "I'd better go now."

"Ssh! Wait until she's finished singing," Ann whispered. For once Jay was looking very smart; his grey trousers were immaculate, his white shirt crisp and clean, his spotted bow tie correctly tied. His hair had been well brushed and his black shoes shone. When Jay did dress up he did it in style.

Miss Bridger had a pleasant but very soft voice and it was difficult to hear her over the band. She came breathlessly to the end of her song and was rewarded with more loud applause and several approving whistles. As she was awarded her medallion, Jay wriggled off the chair and sped away to await his big moment.

Ann smiled at Emma who leaned across and said "I'm keeping my fingers crossed for him."

"Didn't you want to take part?" Ann asked.

Emma shook her head emphatically. "I'd die of fright!" she said.

"Well, ladies and gentlemen," cried Bob Stuart, "wasn't that terrific? I knew you'd enjoy that. Now, by way of a change, we have Abel Hutt from Wyoming, USA. He tells me he's seventy-nine but you won't believe it when you see him. He's got a little monologue about the Wild West – so, let's hear it, ladies and gentlemen. Abel Hutt from Wyoming!"

There was loud applause as a tall, white-haired man ambled out into the spotlight. He wore a large white stetson and looked entirely at ease. He swept off his hat, said "Howdy, one and all," put it back on his head and launched into his monologue which was all about a lonesome cowboy on a lonesome trail.

Ann tried to concentrate but her thoughts returned again and again to the problem of Bourn. She wondered uneasily about Alan and hoped he would not do anything rash without consulting first with her and Luke.

The monologue earned rapturous applause and

99

Mr Hutt retired with the coveted medallion and a broad grin.

Now it was Jay's turn. Emma and Ann exchanged amused glances and sat up in their seats.

Bob Stuart picked up the microphone. "That was an act that will be hard to follow but we have just the man to do it. He is Jason Burnside, only eight years old. He tells me he is from Hastings, England *and* New York – "

There was a ripple of laughter.

"And he is going to sing 'The Teddy Bears Picnic'. So – a big hearty welcome for the little lad himself!"

The audience began to clap enthusiastically but there was no sign of Jay.

Emma shouted, "Come on Jay!"

Ann grinned. "Oh, Jay knows how to make a dramatic entrance," she said. "Keep the audience waiting. Build up the suspense."

Bob Stuart smiled and said, "A slight hiccup, ladies and gentlemen. Excuse me," and went backstage to look for his missing performer.

Emma said, "Perhaps he's gone all bashful."

Ann shook her head. "Not Jay," she said "But I wonder what he's up to."

The ghost of a suspicion entered her mind and her smile faded.

"Perhaps he's rushed off to the toilet," Emma suggested

"It's possible," said Ann.

The nagging suspicion persisted. Bob Stuart returned looking puzzled.

"Well, ladies and gentlemen, it seems we have temporarily mislaid Master Burnside but I'm sure he'll be back with us before long. So we'll go on to the next act which you are going to *love*. It's two little sisters playing a piano duet. They are Caroline West, aged eleven and her sister, Angela, who is two years younger. Let's give them a big hand!"

The two girls walked onto the stage hand in hand while Ann counted to ten and told herself not to panic. Of *course* Jay was all right. He would no doubt be next – but Adam Bourn's words suddenly returned to her. "Let's hope nothing worse happens." Was this the "something worse"?

The sisters played their piece and were followed in due course by a comedian with a terrible repertoire of unfunny jokes. When his place was taken by a conjurer Ann's suspicions hardened into certainty. Something had happened to Jay. She leaned over to Emma and said, "I'm going to look for him. Will you wait here or come with me?"

"I'll come with you," said Emma, seeing that Ann was worried.

Backstage they found a group of people nervously awaiting their turn. Three women were dressed as gipsies and carried tambourines. A young man was juggling with three oranges. Ann asked them about Jay but no one knew what had happened to him. One lady said she thought she saw him talking to a tall man but she couldn't be sure. Ann's heart sank. She spoke to Bob Stuart but he could add nothing more to the little she had already gleaned.

"No one actually saw him go," he told her, "but he can't come to much harm. Probably got stage fright."

"Stage fright!" cried Ann. "But Jay's a born show off! He loves the limelight."

"Well, I'm sorry I can't help you," he said. "We'll keep an eye open for him. But don't worry. He won't come to any harm."

Ann did not share Bob Stuart's confidence and the next half an hour was one of the longest in her life. Together she and Emma set off to search the ship. They looked in both restaurants, the second lounge and the theatre; they tried the casino (out of bounds to children but a remote possibility); the games room, card room and library; the lido, the gallery shops, the health spa and the gymnasium. They had no luck. They braved the bad weather and walked all the decks with the same lack of success. They even tried the Bank, Purser's Office and Travel Bureau. There was no sign of him and by this time they were both thoroughly alarmed.

Ann asked everyone she met – "Have you seen a small boy with a spotted bow tie?" But he seemed to have vanished into thin air.

Emma glanced at Ann's stricken face and said, "Let's go and tell my father."

Ann nodded, unable to trust herself to speak. She felt choked with apprehension and there were tears pricking at her eyelids.

Alan looked up as they entered his cabin, and seeing Ann's shocked expression, cried, "What's happened?"

Quickly Ann told him about Jay's disappearance and he swore under his breath. But at that moment there was a knock at the door.

Alan relaxed. "Guess who?" he said.

"Jay!" cried Ann, weak with relief, and turned to open the door. But it was not Jay who stepped into the cabin, it was Adam Bourn. For a moment nobody spoke.

Then Bourn said. "Ah, Mr Kaufman I believe, or is it Mr Brent of the *New York Times*?"

Ann cried, "If you hurt Jay I'll– "

"You'll what?" he asked. "Shoot me? Hang me? Poison me?"

"Send you back to prison!" she said. "He's only eight. He hasn't done you any harm."

Alan said, "Have you got the boy?"

Bourn assumed an air of great innocence. "Boy? What boy?"

103

"Have you got her brother?" Alan demanded fiercely. "Because if you have – "

Bourn turned his coldly glittering eyes towards him.

"Idle threats, Mr Brent. Idle threats," he said. "What would I want with Miss Burnside's brother?"

"A trade," snapped Alan. "The boy for our silence."

"Oh, you do learn quickly," said Bourn. "Well, perhaps I should explain the situation." He sat down in the armchair and drew the beretta from his pocket. "Now, if you'll all sit down – " he suggested, "and I don't advise any heroics. This is not a toy and it's loaded."

Ann wanted to leap at him and claw his eyes out, but instead she sat down on the bed next to Emma and put an arm round her. Alan sat on the other bed and they all waited helplessly.

"I'm not saying I have the boy," Bourn began, "but let's suppose I do. Let's suppose I need a hostage and I have chosen Jason. Let's suppose I have hidden him away somewhere— "

"You hateful pig!" cried Emma, her face chalky white. Bourn leaned forward and slapped her across the face.

"That's enough from you!" he said. "Keep out of it."

Alan had jumped to his feet but at once the gun turned his way and Ann cried, "Oh don't,

Alan! Please! Let's hear what he has to say."

"A sensible young lady," said Bourn, settling back once more in his chair. "Where was I? Oh yes, *if* I had the young man in safe keeping I could offer you what Mr Brent so accurately calls a trade. You see, thanks to this young busybody – " He glanced at Ann " – you all know too much about my activities and no doubt you're planning to try and stop me. Now, it's really very simple. If you tell *anybody* about what I'm doing, you will never see your brat of a brother again. And make no mistake about it – I do mean never. And no one will be able to prove anything against me. I've been far too clever for that. So what would you gain by denouncing me to the authorities?" His lips parted in a slow, cold smile. "I *might* go back to prison, or I might be acquitted – you have no real evidence – but whatever happened to me, *you* – " he stabbed a finger in Ann's direction " – would never know what happened to your brother. And I think you might miss him."

Ann swallowed hard. She was trying to think but her mind was paralysed with fear.

Bourn looked round at them and it seemed to Ann that his eyes had the malevolent gleam of a snake about to strike.

Alan said. "So, you're admitting to the fraud, are you?"

"Fraud?" said Bourn. "A nasty word."

"Swindle, then," said Alan harshly. "I mean the patches. It's just a way of persuading people to part with their money, isn't it?"

"Only those who can easily afford it," Bourn said smoothly. "You must admit it's rather neat. Foolproof, I thought, until this meddling little fool – " he glanced at Ann and she heard the menace in his voice " – and her precious boyfriend – and then you!" He looked at Alan. "I never did like journalists. Always probing and prying. Never take 'No' for an answer. Always after 'the story'."

"I didn't send you to prison," Alan told him. "I had no argument with you directly. It was the company. It wasn't my fault that they made you the scapegoat."

"But if you hadn't persisted with your claims– "

"Your drug *killed* my wife!"

Bourn controlled his temper with an effort. "Your damned claims ruined me, Mr Brent. But I've served my sentence. In the eyes of society I've atoned for my debt. Now I have to put together a new life and this is my way of doing it."

Ann prayed that Alan would stop baiting the man. She could not understand why he was deliberately trying to make him angry. Desperate to bring about Jay's release, she was willing to promise anything. In vain, she tried to catch Alan's eye – he seemed determined not to look at her.

"You'll cash the cheques, then," Alan persisted,

106

"change your identity and spend the rest of your life in luxury in South America? Is that it?"

"Something like that," said Bourn. "You're really too smart for your own good, Mr Brent." Abruptly he stood up. "I hope we understand each other. Your brother, Miss Burnside, will be perfectly safe unless one of you does something foolish. Really, all you have to do is carry on normally. You come in to meals— "

"Sharing a table with *you*?" cried Ann. "I couldn't eat. It would choke me."

"Then you'll have to force it down, Miss Burnside," he said. "The stewards might become suspicious if you stay away from meals. And remember, your silence is essential until we have docked in New York and I am ashore."

"But how will we know where to find Jay after you've gone?"

"I'll send you a note."

She said, "But how do we know we can trust you?"

"Oh, you don't," he said. "That's the beauty of it. You don't know. But what alternative have you? You either go to the captain and forfeit your brother's life, or you keep your side of the bargain and hope I keep mine."

"You're an out and out crook!" cried Alan, jumping to his feet. "Suppose we refuse your trade? Then you're finished."

"And so is the brat," Bourn reminded him.

Ann leaned over and touched Alan's hand imploringly.

"Please!" she said. "We must save Jay."

"Yes, Dad, please!" cried Emma, her lips trembling. Slowly Alan sat down again.

"You're learning, Mr Brent," said Bourn. "So, is it understood? If I go free, so does the boy. It's really up to you."

He slipped the gun back into his pocket, opened the door, and stepped outside. They listened in silence to his retreating footsteps and then Emma burst into tears and threw herself into Alan's arms.

Alan looked at Ann over the top of her head.

"I'm sorry if I scared you," he told her gently, "but I had to goad him a little. You see, I had the tape recorder going. We've got it all on tape."

Ten

Ann stared at him. "You mean you were recording everything?"

He nodded, and, with the exaggerated manner of a magician, he pulled a small tape recorder from his pocket and held it up.

"Every word!" he told them. "A full confession, wouldn't you say?"

"That's wonderful, Dad!" cried Emma. "Isn't he clever, Ann!"

They were both looking at Ann who was slowly shaking her head, her expression shocked and disbelieving.

"You can't mean to use that," she said shakily. "After all he said."

"Of course we're going to use it," Alan retorted. "The captain will be convinced when he hears this. End of problem."

"No!" cried Ann. "The *beginning* of the problem. If you take that to the captain we'll never see Jay again. You mustn't do anything to risk Jay's life."

"I wouldn't dream of risking anyone's life," said

Alan quietly. "I don't believe for one moment that Bourn meant what he said. I can recognize bluff when I hear it." Emma looked at him anxiously.

"But suppose he *wasn't* bluffing?" she said.

"Exactly," said Ann with a grateful look at Emma. "We can't know for sure that he was bluffing. I don't think he was. You can't take that tape to the captain, Alan. I won't let you."

Emma's mouth trembled. "I don't want anything to happen to Jay."

"Nothing will," he told her. "Look, do please be sensible, Ann."

"Sensible!" Ann burst out. "Would *you* be sensible if it was Emma he was holding and not Jay?" Her eyes flashed. "You know the sort of man he is. He obviously doesn't like children. Look how quick he was to slap Emma just now. He's a callous monster and he might – he just might – "

She broke off and hid her face in her hands.

Alan said grimly. "All right, then, Ann. Let's imagine the very worst. Suppose he has already killed Jay."

Ann gave a cry of anguish, Emma's head snapped up and both girls stared at Alan in horror.

"I only said *suppose*," he reminded them quickly. "If we do nothing he'll just walk off the ship with his money– "

"Damn and blast the money!" cried Ann. "I don't care about that any more."

"Let me finish," said Alan. "He'll walk off the ship with the money – a thief and a murderer. We have the means to have him arrested but we let him go scot-free. Is that really what you want?"

Ann said bitterly. "So you think we should take a chance and hope for the best? Well, I don't. Jay's my brother and right now he's all I care about."

"Please," begged Emma. "Ann's right. Don't do anything to hurt Jay."

Alan's expression was unrelenting. "I'm sorry," he said. "I understand how you feel but we have to do the right thing." Ann jumped furiously to her feet.

"Right thing for you, perhaps!" she cried furiously. She snatched the tape recorder from Alan's hands, and made a grab for the door.

"Oh no you don't!" he shouted and the next moment they were wrestling together. Ann was fighting to hold on to the recorder and also to open the door but although she fought ferociously, she had no real chance. A few moments later Alan had regained possession of the recorder, Emma was crying and Ann had gone, slamming the door behind her.

Dishevelled and sobbing with frustration, she ran blindly along the passage and up the stairs. People stared at her as she pushed past them. She did not know where she was going or why she was running, except that, perhaps, she wanted to put as great a distance as possible between herself and Alan. Alan – whom she had looked upon as a friend. Had *trusted*. Now she regretted ever having confided in him.

"I wish I'd never met him!" she cried aloud, quite unaware of the effect her appearance was having on the other passengers. She ran on, along another passage and up yet more stairs, until at last, she sank down, breathless and exhausted, in the doorway of one of the gallery shops.

A woman coming out of the shop nearly fell over her and looked down at her, disconcerted.

"Is anything wrong?" she asked. "Oh dear, I can see there is."

Ann looked at her through tear-dimmed eyes. "It's my brother," she whispered.

"Your brother? What's the matter with him?"

She was angular with blue-rinsed hair and clutched several purchases to her. For a second or two Ann longed to blurt out the whole story, but she bit back the flood of words and merely shook her head.

"It's nothing," she said and at once realized how ridiculous that must sound. Somehow she forced the ghost of a smile and stood up.

The woman looked relieved. "Well, if you're sure you're all right," she said.

"Quite sure," said Ann wearily.

As the woman hurried thankfully away, Ann made an effort to think rationally. Of course! There was still Luke. Luke would see things her way. Taking out a handkerchief, she wiped her eyes and blew her nose. She took several deep breaths and then made her way to Luke's cabin and knocked on the door. Luke opened it.

"Thank goodness you've come," he said. "Come in."

"What is it?" she asked, dismayed by his manner.

"It's Sven," Luke told her.

But Ann had already glanced towards the bed and she was at once aware of the dramatic change in the old man. He lay back on the bed, his eyes closed, his face ashen. Without the cheerful smile she knew so well, Sven looked very different. The muscles in his face sagged and his mouth hung open. He looked years older.

"It's that beastly drug," said Luke. "He was rambling away and then he suddenly cried out and collapsed. I tried to rouse him but he was unconscious. I thought he was dead." His words reminded her of Jay's plight but she said nothing.

"I rang for the steward," he went on, "and he fetched the doctor. He came about ten minutes ago. As soon as he saw him he said, 'Not another one!' "

"What! You mean Sven's not the only one?"

"The doctor's got two other cases. Both people who were wearing the patches. One of them is Mrs Bell. Apparently some people are allergic to one of the ingredients in the drug. It brings on a coma."

113

Ann's thoughts swam chaotically.

"Shouldn't Sven be in the hospital?" she asked at last.

He nodded. "They've gone to arrange a bed and then they'll send a stretcher for him. Oh Ann! He looks so ill. I can't bear it. If only I could do something to help him. I keep thinking – suppose he dies."

At that moment they heard footsteps in the corridor and the sound of a wheeled trolley. Luke opened the door and a white-coated orderly said "Gentleman for the hospital? Foreign name I can't remember."

"Yes," said Luke. "It's Hannson."

The orderlies pushed in the trolley and Luke and Ann watched as they lifted Sven from his bed. They laid him gently on the trolley and covered him with a blanket.

"Soon have him nicely tucked up in the hospital," said one of the men cheerfully.

"Thank you," said Luke. "Should I come with him to see him settled in?"

"Up to you, sir."

"Then I will."

They wheeled the trolley out of the cabin and Luke went with them, his eyes never leaving Sven's face.

Dejectedly, Ann followed the little procession as it made its way along the passage, into the lift and down to the hospital. She was thinking hard as she waited outside the hospital for Luke to return. It had been her intention to tell Luke about Bourn's latest move in an effort to win his sympathies for her own case. Now she knew that Luke would take Alan's side. If Bourn's patch killed Sven then he would want him brought to justice and rightly so. For a while she wondered how she could persuade him to see her point of view but the more she thought about it the more uncertain she became.

By the time Luke returned she had come to a decision. After much heart-searching she had changed her mind. She would tell Luke everything and then together they would go back to Alan.

Back in Luke's cabin she poured out the latest events and Luke was shaken.

"So you see," she finished, "we have to take that tape to the captain. For Sven and Jay and poor Mrs Bell. For all of them."

"I guess so," said Luke. "If we don't he will be free to repeat the trick on another ship and then other innocent people will be hurt. I know how you feel about Jay, Ann, but I think if you could ask Jay he'd probably say 'Go get him!'"

Ann laughed tremulously. "Let's go then," she said.

They knocked on Alan's door and as soon as he opened it Emma threw her arms round Ann's neck.

"I didn't think you'd ever speak to us again," she cried. "I was so miserable."

"*I* didn't think I would," Ann told her, "but something else has happened and it's changed my mind. But first I want to apologize. Alan, I'm sorry I behaved the way I did." She turned to Luke. "Now tell them about Sven."

The room was silent while Luke told them about the delayed effect the patches were having, but when he had finished Alan nodded.

"That settles it!" he said. "We go right now."

He was reaching under his pillow for the tape recorder when one of the stewards came to the door with a message to say that the captain wanted to see Ann Burnside in his cabin urgently.

"Me?" she cried.

"I've been looking all over for you," the steward told her. "Then someone remembered they'd seen you and young Emma together at the talent show so I thought I might find you here."

"Wait!" cried Luke. "I've been caught before with these so-called messages." He turned to the startled steward. "Can you prove that the message really came from the captain?"

"Of course, sir," he replied indignantly. "It was the first officer, Mr Fellows, who told me and the captain told him."

"Thanks, Luke," said Ann. "It was sensible to check but I think this time it's genuine."

Luke hesitated but Alan agreed with Ann.

"But I don't think she should go alone," he said. "We'll all go."

The steward looked a trifle unhappy. "The message was only for Miss Burnside," he said.

"Not to worry," Alan told him. "We were all intending to visit the captain before you brought the message."

"Very good, sir."

The captain was astonished to see four people answering his summons, but he asked them politely to sit down.

Ann said. "If it's about Adam May we would all like to hear it, please Captain."

"It *is* about him," the captain told her. He went to his desk and picked up a slip of paper. "This is a message from the British Medical Council," he said. "It corroborates your suspicions about Mr May." He picked up another sheet. "This is from Scotland Yard. It fills in a lot of background. And of course I am now fully aware of the terrible side effects of the drug. It's a ghastly business." He ran a hand through his hair and Ann felt sorry for him. Being the captain of such a ship was a tremendous responsibility. "I'm afraid I owe you an apology, Miss Burnside," he said. "Mr May *is* an imposter. I have wired all details to my company and I am awaiting a decision from them."

Ann nodded gravely. "Mr Kaufman has something

117

you should hear," she said, "but I'm afraid it's even worse than you think. My brother's been kidnapped. Mr May is holding him as a hostage. Mr Kaufman has it all on tape."

The captain gasped. "Kidnapped?" he whispered. "But that's incredible!" He groped for his chair and sat down heavily. Then he nodded to Alan.

"Let me hear the tape," he said.

The recording was far from perfect but it was clear enough to convince the captain that Adam May, alias Bourn, was no less than a callous criminal.

The captain took out a handkerchief and mopped beads of perspiration from his forehead. They all waited in silence as he considered the full significance of what he had heard. At last he turned to Ann.

"Tell me about your brother's disappearance," he said. "How did it happen?"

Ann explained as briefly as she could and when she had finished he shook his head.

"The quicker that man is behind bars the better," he murmured. "He's a menace to society."

"Is there anyone on board who is authorized to arrest him?" asked Luke.

"I am," said the captain. "Actually, any one of the crew or passengers could make a citizen's arrest but I shan't allow them to take that risk. The safety of our passengers is our first priority." He turned to Ann. "I think it unlikely he will have harmed your brother. You see, if his bluff works and you don't report what you know about him, he won't want to be involved in a full-scale murder hunt. Interpol would be alerted and he'd have policemen looking for him wherever he went. He'd have nowhere to hide. All he wants is to find somewhere safe to enjoy his money. So try not to worry too much. We'll find your brother safe and sound."

"I hope you're right," said Ann quietly.

There was a knock at the door. "The reply from the company," said the officer, and the captain told him to wait while he opened it.

"As I expected," he said, and read aloud. "Take all steps necessary stop Safety of passengers imperative stop U.S. police alerted stop They will meet ship and take Bourn into custody stop Notify proceedings most urgent stop Wish all success. End."

The captain introduced the officer as Chief Officer Fenwick who said briskly. "Well, all we have to do now is to nab him. May I volunteer for the job, sir?"

He was a small wiry man with brown hair, greying at the temples, but there was a steely look in his eyes.

"Thank you," said the captain.

"I've been thinking it over since you told me about it, sir," he went on eagerly, "and I'd like to suggest we make the arrest as he comes out of breakfast tomorrow. We could have two men outside the door of the dining room – me and another chap – and we could be in touch with walkie-talkies with one of the steward's inside the room to let us know when he got up from his table."

"He sits with us," said Ann. "Of all people we could share with it had to be him."

The captain frowned. "That will be awkward," he said. "After what's happened. He specifically said you were to carry on normally. If you don't turn up he might wonder where you are and what you're up to and get suspicious."

Luke looked at Ann. "Could you bear it?" he asked. "You could sit in stony silence as though you're furious because he's won."

Alan said, "Of course she can, because it will help to get Jay back."

Impatiently, Chief Officer Fenwick went on with his plan. "As Bourn comes out of the door we grab one arm each and twist it behind his back so that if he's carrying his gun he can't get to it. Then we slip the handcuffs on— "

"You have handcuffs?" said Ann, surprised.

"Oh yes, miss," he told her. "We have to be prepared for every emergency. Well, sir, what do you think?"

There was a long silence while the captain thought through the plan but finally he nodded, to the chief officer's obvious relief.

"Thank you, sir," he said. "I'll get everyone organized. Oh, sir, I think Officer Cray would also like to volunteer."

The captain gave a short laugh. "I rather thought he would," he said. "Yes, that's O.K. with me. He's a good man. Breakfast it is, then."

"Suppose he skips breakfast," said Luke.

"Then we'll make it lunch," said Chief Officer Fenwick.

But the captain shook his head. "No. If he doesn't go in to breakfast, we'll think of something else. We won't delay it further. I want this business over and done with."

"Couldn't you rush his cabin while he's asleep?" Emma suggested.

The captain shook his head. "We daren't risk anything while he's in his cabin in case the young hostage is in there with him."

Alan said, "But when he goes to breakfast – *if* he does – then we could search his room."

"Oh, we will," said the captain. "Now may I suggest you leave the details to us. All we ask of you is that you don't do anything to arouse his suspicions." He glanced at his watch. "Have you eaten?" he asked them. "It's nearly nine thirty." He turned to Ann. "If you don't show up, Bourn will think it's odd."

"I'll go now," she said. She stood up and suddenly held out her hand to Chief Officer Fenwick. "Good luck for tomorrow," she said.

He shook her hand warmly. "Don't worry, miss," he said. "We'll get your brother back for you. That's a promise."

Eleven

Bourn was not at the table when Ann hurried in to dinner and took her seat with the Hubbards and their daughter, who were looking pale but cheerful.

"Too late!" teased Simon. "We're closed!"

"Sorry," said Ann. "I got delayed." She chose pork steaks with cream and Lyonnaise potatoes.

"Where's young Jay then?" asked Mabel.

"He's not feeling too good," Ann lied. "The steward's made him some chicken sandwiches."

"Poor lad," said John. "Never mind, the sea's easing off a bit, thank goodness. Soon we'll all be feeling better. It certainly has been an eventful trip. Lots of excitement. Certainly couldn't be bored on this trip."

Ann nodded. Too much excitement, she thought. More than enough to last her for the rest of her life. Being bored sounded a luxury!

Simon brought her dinner and she discovered to her surprise that she was hungry.

"That awful Mr Bourn came in earlier," Alice confided. "I tried to be pleasant, well we all did, but he's such a misery. If you ask him a question all you get is a nod or a shake of the head."

"Or a grunt," said Mabel. "I just don't like the man."

"Words don't cost anything," said John. "After all, dinner should be a sociable occasion. "Do you like him, Ann?"

Ann nearly choked on a piece of potato. "Like him?" she cried. "No, I don't. I hate him. He's an absolute – " She bit back a very rude word and repeated. "I just hate him, that's all."

Three faces turned towards her in astonishment and she searched her mind for some way to explain her outburst. "He was quite rude to Jay earlier on," she invented.

John shook his head. "Some people have no patience with children. I had a brother-in-law like that. Children brought out the worst in him, if you know what I mean – "

Ann did not feel like talking but fortunately the others did and they chattered on without noticing her subdued mood. They left before she had finished her ice cream and Ann was glad to be alone with her thoughts.

"Tomorrow, I shall have Jay back," she whispered. "Large as life and twice as cheeky!"

Yes, she must cling onto that thought, she told herself, and not allow her fears to get her down. "Breakfast tomorrow," she thought. It was only a

124

few hours away. Less than half a day. If she could only survive until then. But would it all go according to plan?

Tony broke into her thoughts. "I think I shall have a treat for you tomorrow," he said. "Want to try and guess?"

Ann shook her head, too tired to hazard even the most feeble guess.

"I'll be putting the flowers back on the table," he told her. "The weather forecast is good."

"Oh good," said Ann, trying to inject a little enthusiasm into her remark. She no longer cared about the weather. All she could think about was her brother.

Later that evening she played chess with Luke but they were both too worried to give the game much attention. Poor Sven was still in a coma and Luke had telephoned his mother in New York to prepare her for the worst. She would meet the ship when it docked and accompany her husband to hospital.

They parted about eleven and went back to their respective cabins. Try as she would Ann could not sleep and the hours of the night crept by, and in her deep despair it seemed to her that morning would never come.

Eventually it did, however, and she washed and dressed as quickly as she could and arrived at the breakfast table before anyone else was down.

Alice Paine arrived five minutes later saying that her parents were not hungry and Ann waited in an agony of apprehension. Was Bourn going to join them? She was buttering a slice of toast when at last she saw his tall figure making its way towards them.

"Oh dear," whispered Alice, "here comes Misery Guts." He sat down without glancing at either of them. His back was towards the door, Ann noted with satisfaction. Alice looked at Ann meaningfully.

Then she said, "Good morning, Mr May," in a reproving tone. "Sea's much calmer, don't you think?"

Bourn raised his eyes momentarily from the menu and gave her a cold glance but did not trouble to answer her.

Alice flushed at the deliberate snub and muttered, "Well, really! Some people!"

Ann tried to smile at her but her face felt stiff with anxiety. She had tried to pick out the steward who was carrying the walkie-talkie but they all seemed to be carrying on normally and none of them, with the exception of Simon and Tony, even glanced her way.

She had not seen the two ship's officers who should have been outside the dining room door. Presumably they must be keeping out of sight until Bourn made a move to leave the restaurant. She glanced at him surreptitiously but he was eating a dish of stewed apple

126

with apparent unconcern. "You have kidnapped my brother!" she thought furiously, "and made Sven ill and yet you sit there as though you are as normal as the rest of us. I hate you, Adam Bourn. I hate you."

She took a bite of her toast and chewed it but she had to think about the process, consciously moving her jaw and then forcing herself to swallow. The toast slid reluctantly down her dry throat. Suddenly, out of the corner of her eye she saw Chief Officer Fenwick. He was standing outside the door of the restaurant, apparently in earnest conversation with another officer. That would no doubt be Officer Cray, thought Ann.

When Bourn pushed back his chair she saw one of the stewards turn away and take something from his pocket. So *he* was the lookout with the walkie-talkie! Alice was saying something to her but Ann could not hear for the hammering of her heart.

Bourn strode towards the door and Ann watched breathlessly. She saw the two ship's officers part company – Chief Officer Fenwick stood looking out of the window at the sea. The other man was out of sight, hidden by the door.

As Bourn went out through the door, Ann half rose in her seat, her fingers crossed behind her back.

"Please! *Please*!" she whispered.

"Ann? What is it?" said Alice. "Ann! I'm talking to you."

127

Ignoring her, Ann began to hurry after Bourn. He had stepped through the doorway and was out of sight. She began to run, aware suddenly of a commotion outside the restaurant. She heard raised voices, a thud and then a woman began to scream. A shot rang out.

"Please let them catch him!" cried Ann as she reached the dining room door.

There she saw a scene of utter confusion. Bourn was on the ground and Officer Cray was pinned beneath him. Chief Officer Fenwick lay sprawled below the window, apparently unconscious and with blood oozing from a wound in his neck. A woman passenger had been knocked over in the fight and a man was helping her to her feet. A potted palm tree lay on its side, spilling earth onto the green carpet.

"Out of the way, please!"

The steward with the walkie-talkie raced past Ann and leapt onto Bourn's back, pulling him off his victim. The walkie-talkie slid along the floor.

Officer Cray shouted. "For God's sake keep back everyone. He's got a gun."

Bourn now held the gun in one hand and as he struggled with the steward it went off again, fortunately hitting no one but shattering the window above Chief Officer Fenwick who slowly opened his eyes. When he realized what was happening, he struggled to his knees but he was bleeding copiously and Ann ran forward to tell him he was in no fit state to take further action. Before she reached him, however, he collapsed again, his eyes closed.

By this time Bourn had managed to throw off his attacker and was backing away, menacing everyone around him with the revolver.

"Keep back!" he warned. He caught sight of Ann and his face reddened with rage. "So, it was you, you stupid little fool. I warned you – "

Ann's throat was dry but she took a few steps towards him.

"Where's Jay? Just tell me where he is."

But Bourn turned and ran away, zig-zagging through the startled passengers in the Queen's Room, making for the great curved staircase.

Officer Cray had staggered to his feet and now began to run after him, shouting desperately, warning everyone not to interfere. Ann felt as though the whole scene was being enacted in slow motion.

Ignoring the officer's warning, she, too, began to run after Bourn as he mounted the main staircase with Cray and the steward close behind him. When Bourn reached the gallery, he turned right and his pursuers did the same. Ann turned left with the idea of heading him off. It worked exactly as she thought. Bourn was so busy looking over his shoulder he failed to see her until there were only twenty feet between them. To her horror he aimed the gun at her and pulled the trigger. As Ann ducked, she heard the bullet whistle past her head and smash

129

into the window of the duty free kiosk behind her. In that instant Bourn passed her, running towards the door which would take him onto the open deck. Ann recovered and straightened up as Cray and the steward ran past her. She followed them out onto the deck in time to see Bourn climb up on the rail. He clung there briefly, screaming abuse at them, then he swung his legs over and held onto the outside of the rail. The wind tugged at his hair and clothes and below him the ship's foaming wake curled through the grey-green water and spray glistened in the air around him.

"Grab him!" shouted Officer Cray.

As the two men raced forward, Bourn raised the gun to his own head, and pulled the trigger. There was a muffled report and then he fell back, away from the ship, his body twisting, his arms outstretched.

Ann ran forward and clutched the rail. Below her, held by the waves, she saw his body. Briefly a small red stain spread out from his head, then a bigger wave carried him from sight. He reappeared again but the ship was moving at a tremendous speed and within seconds he was lost to view.

Dizzy and shaking with shock, Ann forced herself back from the rail, afraid that she would lose her balance and follow Bourn into the cold green sea. So he was gone – killed by his own hand. She was glad and yet with his death the hate she had felt earlier had evaporated. She sighed as Officer Cray put an arm round her and led her back inside again.

All around the gallery people stood in excited groups, wondering what was happening.

"Jay!" whispered Ann. "We must find Jay."

At that moment Luke ran up, followed by the captain.

"They've found him!" cried Luke and threw his arms round her in a hug of triumph. "He was in Bourn's wardrobe, unconscious."

"Unconscious! Oh no! What happened to him? Is he going to be all right? Where is he?"

Luke released her, smiling, and she began to relax.

"One question at a time," said Luke. "He's in the hospital, but recovering. He's not really unconscious, just sleeping heavily. They reckon Bourn gave him an injection of something to keep him quiet. So now we know what the syringe was that Alan found. A nasty little trick for emergencies. When Jay wakes up he probably won't remember a thing."

"Thank heavens!" cried Ann. The relief was overwhelming. "I must go down to the hospital to see him."

"Hold on a minute," said Luke. "What happened up here? Have they got Bourn?"

"No," said Ann soberly. "He shot himself."

Chief Officer Cray filled in the rest of the details and Luke whistled. Ann turned to the captain.

131

"Aren't we going back to recover Bourn's body?" she asked.

The captain shook his head. "We'd never find it," he said. "The ship is travelling so fast we'd be miles away before we could stop. If we described a circle the body would be long gone before we could reach the spot where he went in. And the current has to be taken into consideration. That will carry him off course. No, there's no going back. After all, he didn't fall in. He went deliberately. He wanted a watery grave and that's what he got."

Ann was silent but then Alan and Emma apppeared and all the news had to be repeated for their benefit. Ann asked after Sven and learned that there was a slight improvement. He had opened his eyes several times but had made no attempt to speak and seemed to hear nothing that was said to him. Mrs Bell *had* improved. She was fully conscious.

Alan rubbed his hands together delightedly. "What a story!" he said. "The ship's company will no doubt be pleased at the way it's ended. They wouldn't have enjoyed a long trial. Bad for its image. Still, they'll have a barrage of reporters to deal with in New York. This little lot will be headlines all over the world. Can you imagine a drama-cum-disaster on one of the world's biggest liners? Everyone will be talking about it – until a new disaster occurs somewhere else and then it will be forgotten. Very fickle, the public."

132

Luke said. "I suppose this is a real scoop for you. I mean, you're probably the only journalist on the ship."

Alan nodded and his eyes gleamed. "That's right. This is my scoop. An exclusive story. It's what every journalist dreams about. I'll probably write another book and make our fortune." He ruffled Emma's hair. "How's about that, Emma? Do you think you'd like being rich? I'll buy you that pony you've always wanted."

Ann tried not to think too harshly of him. He was a journalist and he had to think this way. People's lives had been ruthlessly disrupted and a man had killed himself but to Alan it was simply the scoop of his life. The long awaited exclusive. He would even write a book about it, turning people's fears and heartaches into a "good read". With all the horrors still fresh in her mind, she found it difficult to accept that Alan might see it all in a different light. He caught her eye at that moment and somehow read in her expression the essence of what she was thinking and for a moment his smile wavered. But then he grinned.

"Look, it's all over now," he said defensively. "All over bar the shouting, as they say. What d'you expect me to do, Ann? It's my job."

Ann bit back a sharp retort and said only, "Yes, I know."

133

Emma looked at her anxiously. "It's all right now, isn't it, Ann?"

"Yes," said Ann.

Luke snapped his fingers suddenly and said, "We didn't get the cheques back! They must still be in his jacket – the one he's wearing."

Alan roared with laughter. "He's not going to cash them in Davy Jones's locker!" he reminded them. "I don't think we need to worry on that score. None of his victims will lose a penny. But I shouldn't be standing around here chatting. I must make a few phone calls. Get a photographer to meet the ship. Maybe we could get Jay to curl up in the wardrobe, the way he was when they found him – " He caught Ann's cold gaze and said hastily. "No, maybe not. Never mind." And hurried away.

Ann turned to Luke. "Chief Officer Fenwick was injured," she said. "I'm going to the hospital to ask after him and to see Jay."

"I'll come with you," he said.

Twelve

As they went into the hospital, a nurse met them and Ann enquired about Chief Officer Fenwick.

"He's a very lucky man," she told them. "Another half inch and the bullet would have severed his spine. Very lucky indeed. As it is, he's lost a lot of blood but we've given him a transfusion. He'll pull through, don't you worry." She smiled at Ann. "I expect you want to have a peep at that young brother of yours. He's still asleep but the doctor doesn't want to try and rouse him. He's had a terrible experience and sleep is a good healer of minds as well as bodies."

She led the way into a small room and Luke and Ann tiptoed in behind her. Jay looked like a ghost — his face was pale, his mouth drooped and there were grey shadows under his eyes. Ann felt a lump in her throat as she reached forward and picked up one of his hands which lay outside the counterpane.

"Jay," she whispered. "Good to have you back."

The nurse said, "He looks worse than he is. Don't fret. He'll bob up some time tomorrow as good as new."

"He's alive," said Ann. "That's the main thing. Maybe I should sit with him until he wakes, then he'll see me and won't be too upset. Otherwise he'll wonder where he is."

The nurse shook her head vigorously. "He's not likely to wake until tomorrow," she said. "That's what the doctor said. Come back tomorrow, early as you like."

Luke said, "How's Sven?"

The nurse at once assumed a more professional manner and said briskly, "As well as can be expected."

"That doesn't mean anything," he protested. "Is he better or worse?"

"He's stable," she said. "His condition is satisfactory."

Luke looked at Ann and opened his mouth to speak but she hastily put a hand on his arm. "If he's no worse, Luke, that's good," she said. "Can we see him, nurse, please?"

The nurse agreed a trifle reluctantly and they followed her into another smaller room where Sven lay exactly as Ann had seen him before. Stable? Was that the word for it? Suppose he never did come out of the coma? That wretched Bourn, she thought. And yet – she thought suddenly of Bourn's father and mother and imagined them hearing news of his death and the events leading up to it. Somehow they would try not to believe it. Somehow they would still have to see Adam as the promising young son of whom they were once so proud. To his parents he would never be a callous, unscrupulous criminal. It was all terribly sad.

"A penny for them," said Luke.

She shook her head. "It doesn't matter," she said with a sigh. "Do you want to stay with Sven or are you going back to your cabin?"

"No point in you staying," said the nurse firmly.

So they both went away, leaving Jay and Sven in her capable hands.

Next morning the *Santa Lucia* docked in New York harbour, nudged into her berth by two small tugs. Passengers lined the rails with cameras and videos to record their arrival amongst the city's skyscrapers. The ship was only five hours late for they had made up some of the lost time on the previous day. Ann had woken early after a refreshing night's sleep and, washed and dressed, had made her way back to the hospital. To her immense relief, Jay was already stirring.

"He's been singing," said the nurse. "'The Teddy Bears Picnic', over and over. I know the blessed words by heart now." She laughed and began to sing. "If you go down to the woods tonight you'd better be on your guard – "

Ann smiled. "That's what he was going to sing at the talent show," she said, "before he was kidnapped. He'll be so cross he hasn't got another medallion to add to his collection."

Ann pulled up a chair and sat beside the bed. There was more colour in Jay's face and his eyelids flickered. She sat there for perhaps ten minutes and then suddenly, without warning, he opened his eyes and stared round wonderingly. Then he turned to Ann and frowned.

"Where is this place?" he asked. "I don't like it."

She explained as simply as she could, choosing her words carefully, wondering how much, if anything, he would remember of his ordeal.

The nurse popped her head round the door and, seeing that he was awake, went off to notify the doctor.

Jay was struggling to sit up when he arrived and did not take kindly to being examined.

"You had a bit of a rough time, old lad," the doctor told him when he was satisfied that he had suffered no lasting effects from his adventure. "Can you remember what happened?"

Jay screwed up his face with concentration. "It was that man," he said. "The one at our table. He wouldn't let me sing my song. He said he had some real medals and I could choose one I wanted. He got hold of my arm and kept pulling me. He said they were much better than the talent show medals. I told him I mustn't go with strangers but he said he wasn't a stranger because I knew him because he sits

138

at our table. He said he had a German medal called the Iron Cross." He looked up at Ann indignantly. "When I got to his cabin there weren't any medals at all and he tied my hands together. I kicked him as hard as I could but he stuck a needle in my arm. I didn't cry but I hate him. He's a liar. I'm glad I kicked him. Can I go and sing my song now?"

The doctor explained that he had been asleep for a very long time and had missed the show but he promised to ask the captain if he could have a medal for not crying when the needle went into his arm. Jay cheered up and half an hour later, after a light breakfast of eggs and toast he was allowed to get up.

The press, alerted by Alan's phone call, were waiting on the quayside and had obtained permission to board the ship before the passengers disembarked. Ann and Jay had been warned and had agreed to be interviewed. The captain invited them into his stateroom and Alan, Luke and Emma were there also. Cameramen and a three-man television crew also squeezed into the room, but after a great deal of confusion they were finally ready to start.

First the captain read a brief account of the events of the last few days and expressed the company's deep regret for the distress caused to its passengers.

Jay was then asked some questions which he answered, but his main grievance was that he had missed taking part in the talent show. The captain then stepped forward.

"The company feels that Master Jay Burnside has behaved with great fortitude throughout his ordeal and would like to present him with this medallion as a token of their esteem."

Ann nudged him and Jay stepped forward. The captain handed over the medallion and there was a round of applause.

Jay thanked the captain then turned to face the cameras.

"Ladies and gentlemen," he began.

"Oh no!" cried Ann. "You don't have to make a speech, Jay."

But Jay was not going to miss his moment of glory before the television cameras.

"I just want to say that this is a smashing ship," he said, "and the captain is smashing, too. And the games room," he added as an afterthought.

Then he went back to his seat and it was Ann's turn. She found herself facing a bewildering barrage of questions.

"How did you feel when you discovered your brother had been kidnapped?"

"Terrible," she said. "I felt very frightened at the thought I might not see him again."

"What are your feelings towards Adam Bourn?"

She hesitated. "Now I feel sorry for him. Almost . . . but not quite."

"Did you see him shoot himself?"

"Yes," said Ann. "I hope one day I shall be able to forget it. It was horrible."

"Would events have been different if the captain had believed you when you first told him of your suspicions?"

A tricky question, that, thought Ann, with the captain's eye on her.

"I can't say," she said, "But I do know that the captain and crew of the *Santa Lucia* have been marvellous. I can't praise them enough."

"Will you ever travel on this ship again?"

"Of course I will!" she cried. "Whenever I can."

Eventually, it was Luke's turn. He told them that his stepfather was still in a coma but that Mrs Bell and the other patients were well on the way to recovery. Ann, he said generously, should get most of the credit. She had been the first to suspect that anything was wrong.

Alan then announced that he would answer no questions as his full account would appear in the *New York Times* and would include a full transcript of the tape recording he had made of their conversation with Bourn.

And that, the captain said firmly, was enough. There was work to do. Someone asked him if the ship would be late setting sail for her return crossing.

"Not if we can help it!" he answered grimly.

He explained that they had to see hundreds of passengers ashore, clean the ship, take on fresh provisions and then take hundreds of new passengers on board. It would have to be the fastest "turn-around" the ship had ever undertaken. There was no more time for the press. The conference was at an end.

Grumbling among themselves, the press reluctantly departed and Jay and Ann said "Goodbye" to Alan and Emma. Then Ann exchanged telephone numbers with Luke.

"We will see you again, won't we?" said Ann. "You do promise to keep in touch. We must know what happens to Sven and – I'd hate to think I wouldn't see you again. I was so lucky, meeting you. I never could have survived these last few days without your help."

"Of course we'll see each other again," he assured her. "I'll telephone you. I'm sure my mother will want to meet you. You and Jay will have to spend a weekend with us."

Jay said. "I could sing you my song."

"I'll look forward to that," said Luke with a wink for Ann. "Now I've got to sort out my luggage and Sven's. My mother is going to come on board to wait for Sven's ambulance."

"Well," said Ann, "it's 'Goodbye' for now."

She looked at Luke and he must have read her

142

thoughts because he stepped forward and kissed her.
"Be seeing you," he said.

"Ooh!" cried Jay, his eyes as round as saucers.
"I'm telling!"

Luke and Ann laughed and then Luke shook
hands with Jay and told him not to get into any
more scrapes.

There was no time for any more. A steward
arrived for Luke to say his mother was with the
captain and Ann and Jay hurried away to collect
their luggage and make their own way down the
gangway. On the quayside, to their great relief,
they found their father waiting to welcome them
home.

Two weeks later Ann and Jay spent the weekend with Luke's family in their penthouse suite on
Fifth Avenue where they found Sven at home and
recovering slowly but surely. He greeted them with
affection and seemed little the worse for his terrible
ordeal. All in all the affair had ended better than
any of them had dared to hope – but it had been
a voyage none of them would ever forget.